COUNTERFEIT MAGIC

KELLEY ARMSTRONG

SUBTERRANEAN PRESS 2010

First Edition

ISBN
978-1-59606-328-0

Subterranean Press
PO Box 190106
Burton, MI 48519

www.subterraneanpress.com

Home
Sweet
Home

"Cortez-Winterbourne Investigations. How may I help you?"
I smiled as Savannah's voice echoed down the hall.
Even the fake-cheerful lilt was a welcome sound.

Cortez-Winterbourne Investigations. Not the Lucas Cortez
Agency. Not even Cortez and Associates. After three days of
being treated like my husband's assistant, it was good to come
home and hear my own name.

Lucas had been on a case when his father called. Emergency
meeting at Cabal headquarters in Miami. Could Lucas attend?
No? How about me, then? I'd gone with some trepidation, but
Benicio had treated me as his son's partner, soliciting my opinions and listening to them. Unfortunately, he was the only one
who had.

"Paige!" Adam swung out from his office. "Damn, I'm glad
to see you."

"Laptop on the fritz again?"

"Yep. I put it in your office. When can I expect it back?"

I launched a knockback spell, but he ducked it, then followed me into the meeting room. Adam and I have been friends forever, and joined the agency as soon as it opened. His business card says "investigator." That's not untrue—in an agency this size everyone does investigative work. Adam's official position, though, is head of research. Yes, he's the librarian. And when Savannah put that on his cards, he used his half-demon powers to light them on fire. Anyone seeing them would think it was a joke, anyway. With sun-bleached light brown hair, an athletic build, a year-round tan and blazing grin, Adam looks like the only thing he should be researching is new techniques for his surf-board.

"How was Miami?" he asked.

"They asked me to serve coffee again."

Savannah strode in. "I hope you dumped it over their heads this time."

"No, I simply suggested that was a task better suited to the administrative staff. And on that note, a tea would be wonderful."

She snorted and plunked into a chair. That was the problem with having a twenty-one-year-old admin assistant who used to be your ward—a definite lack of proper employee respect. Adam was a little more cognizant of proper conduct, maybe because I've been bossing him around since we were kids. When I hinted at a tea, he poured me a cup of steaming water, passed it over and flipped me a tea bag.

I smiled. "It's good to be in charge again."

"Yeah?" Savannah said. "Well, don't get too comfy, boss. You have a new client arriving in five minutes. Plus, I put a pile of managerial work on your desk."

"As long as you don't ask me to check with Lucas before I do any of it. For three days, I couldn't go five minutes without hearing, 'Shouldn't you run that past your husband?' and, 'What's his opinion?' and, 'Are you sure you're authorized to answer for him?' "

"Condescending bastards," Savannah said. "I'd have smoked 'em with an energy bolt."

"Didn't Benicio stand up for you?" Adam said.

"He did." Which only made things worse. I didn't want my father-in-law defending me. I wanted the Cabal board of directors to hear my opinions and say, "Hmm, she has a point." It had been three years since a family crisis forced Lucas to start playing a role in the Cabal. Three years of trying to prove myself. Yet no matter how hard I worked, nothing changed.

I kicked off my shoes and took a long sip of tea. "I'm just happy to be home, where people actually want *me*, not Lucas. So, there's a client coming?"

"Er, right." Savannah got to her feet. "Actually, I don't know what I was thinking, telling her to come by as soon as your plane landed. You're tired. Let me reschedule—"

"No. I've had my pity party. Getting back to work is the best thing for me."

"Hello?" a woman's voice called.

"She's here?" I said.

"Apparently," Savannah muttered. "She's a Tripudio"—a low-level teleporting half-demon—"so I had to break the wards before she came by earlier."

"And you forgot to reactivate them?" Adam said. "Nice one."

"Hey, even *I* wouldn't be rude enough to teleport through someone's front door."

"Hello?" the voice called again.

Savannah strode into the hall. "Oh, hello, Ms. Cookson. I'm sorry, I didn't hear you ring the buzzer. I'd really suggest you do that next time. We have some seriously nasty security on this place and I'd *hate* to see you—"

"Is he here?"

"Mr. Cortez isn't available, but—"

"I thought you said he'd be here."

"No, I said you could come by for a case intake session. Ms. Winterbourne will be handling that."

"Who?"

I stepped into the hall. The woman was younger than I'd have guessed by her voice. No more than a year or two older than Savannah. Tall, blond, slender and fashionably dressed. And, judging by the way she was squinting at me, in serious need of glasses. The scowl on her face didn't do her any favors either.

"Paige Winterbourne," I said, extending my hand.

She looked at it, then back at me. "Oh. The wife."

"No, the *partner*," Adam said, coming out of the meeting room.

"The *boss*," Savannah said. "The woman who will decide whether we take your case or—"

I stopped them both with a look, then said, "Lucas is away until later this afternoon, so—"

"I'll wait." She sailed past Adam and into a meeting room chair. "I take my coffee black."

"And bitter, I'm sure," Savannah muttered under her breath. She raised her voice so Ms. Cookson could hear. "There's a coffee maker right behind you. It does a cup at a time. Very easy to use. You may want an espresso, though, to keep you awake. It'll be a while before Lucas gets here and even longer before he's ready to talk to you. He's been away from his wife for a week, so he'll want to...visit first."

I shot Savannah another look. I got a look, too—from Ms. Cookson. A slow once-over that said, really, she couldn't imagine why Lucas would bother. Now she was just being a bitch.

I walked to the coffee maker. "Mild, medium or dark roast? We have flavored, too. French vanilla and hazelnut cream."

"His," Savannah said, shooting a thumb at Adam. "He's such a girl."

I waved them off. Savannah went. Adam lingered, giving me a look that said I should be kicking this girl out, not making her coffee. That was his way. Savannah's, too. Yet when people insult and underestimate me, it only makes me all the more determined to prove myself.

It's not as if being overshadowed by my husband is anything new. Even back when I was Coven leader and Lucas was an unemployed lawyer, he was still the one whose name made people sit up and take notice.

My father-in-law is the CEO of the most powerful Cabal in the country. Lucas is his illegitimate youngest son. He's also the one Benicio had named his heir, despite the fact that Lucas had devoted his adult life to fighting Cabal injustices. Pretty hard to compete with that reputation. So I've never tried. I believe in his cause—helping supernaturals—and I joined him knowing I'd always be "that witch who married Lucas Cortez."

When we'd opened the agency, he'd wanted to flip a coin to see whose name went first. I'd refused. He was the renowned crusader. He was the one clients came to see. I understood that, and I'd built up my own reputation until it was a rare customer who insisted on having Lucas handle his case.

Then came the night everything changed. Lucas's two oldest brothers had been murdered, leaving only Carlos, whose greed and amorality might make him a decent Cabal leader if he wasn't so damned incompetent.

Benicio needed help. Benicio needed Lucas.

There'd been a time when Lucas would have let the Cabal crumble. Now he was older, no less idealistic but more realistic, and he'd come to realize that as corrupt as the family business was, it was the best of the North American Cabals. If it failed, the supernatural world would suffer.

Lucas still refused to claim the role of heir, but he did play a role in that family business. Within those misogynistic halls, any credibility I'd gained in the supernatural world was lost. I wasn't just a woman; I was a witch, the lowest of the low, tolerated only because Benicio insisted on it.

As Lucas's star rose, mine tumbled, the effects rippling even back here to the agency.

"I want to speak to Lucas," Ms. Cookson said as I handed her a coffee.

"You will. When he gets here. But we'll be working your case together—"

"I want Lucas."

"You'll have him." I forced a smile. "But it's a package—"

"*Only* Lucas."

I opened her file. "May I call you Ava?" I continued before she could protest. "Although Lucas and I are partners, there are tasks that only one of us handles. Legal work, for example. He's a lawyer; I'm not. Technical work is my forte. I'm a computer programmer; he's not. Beyond those obvious differences, there are tasks one of us does to reduce conflict and confusion. Such as case intake. While clients may—and often do—present a potential case to Lucas personally, I'm the one who decides which ones we take."

"I bet you like that, don't you?"

"The power of choosing the cases? Hardly. We usually evaluate them together and—"

"I mean the power to get rid of clients you don't like. Ones who might pose a threat to your...position."

It took me a moment to get her meaning. When I did, I laughed. I didn't mean to; I just couldn't help it. Her eyes slitted, her lips thinning to a scarlet line.

"Um, no," I said. "Sorry, but no. I'm happy to consider your case, Ava. But I need to know what that case is, so I can present it to Lucas when he returns and give him my recommendation."

She continued to eye me, like a cat that suspects it's being teased. She shifted in her chair. Then, slowly, she began to talk.

Hedging
A Bet

*A*va Cookson was twenty-two. Unmarried. High school education. Lived in Los Angeles. Worked in a clothing store. Had a brother two years her junior. She didn't tell me any of this—it came from the intake form, including a little notation Savannah had made by the name of the store Ava worked at—"overpriced crap made in sweathouses and marketed as designer." All that was incidental...except the last fact.

One brother. Two years her junior. Attended San Francisco State. Or he did, until his body washed up on the shore near Santa Cruz.

"He was murdered," Ava said. "And it's my fault."

Ava was a half-demon, meaning her brother didn't share her demonic father or her powers. He wouldn't have known what she was. That's the theory, anyway.

"He found out," she said. "He caught me teleporting once. You can't explain away something like that."

Which is why you have to be very, very careful.

"You think that's what got him killed," I said.

Her eyes flashed. "Of course not. Don't accuse me—"

"I'm not accusing you of anything. We investigate cases involving the supernatural world, so I presume his entry into that world—through you—somehow resulted in his death."

"Maybe. But Jared was in other trouble, too. He made the wrong kind of friends in college. At first, it was just innocent stuff, like poker for cash pots. But then it was serious gambling. He owed money."

That would seem a more obvious cause of death, but I only nodded, encouraging her to continue.

"I told him I might know a way for him to make money fast. I'd heard of this fight club outside Santa Cruz. For supernaturals. They're always looking for women, especially hot girls, so I figured I could help Jared win his money back. They don't even ask what your power is. That's part of the challenge. I can teleport— not far, but far enough to avoid getting hit. It seemed so easy."

It always does.

"It would have been, too," she continued. "Only they cheated. They set me up against this chick who actually knew how to fight." Imagine that. "I did fine for the first few rounds, but then I started getting tired, and I couldn't teleport as fast. So she won."

I could have seen that one coming a mile away.

"So I'm talking to Jared afterwards and my mouth is bleeding and swelling up, and I'm telling him how sorry I am, and he's saying it's okay. Then this guy walks over, thumps him on the back and congratulates him. Says he didn't get too much—the odds were bad—but winning his first bet is always a good sign."

Ava looked up, eyes blazing. "My *brother* bet *against* me. I stormed out. He came running after me...to hand me the car keys. Tells me he's going to watch a few more rounds, and I can drive the rental car back to the hotel. So I did drive it. All the way back to L.A. Three days later, the rental company calls. The car was in Jared's name, but his credit card is being refused. I call to give him hell, and I can't get hold of him. I figure he's just avoiding me, so I pay the rental company. A month later, someone found his body."

That was the summary. Now I needed details. I took her back to the beginning—when had she told him she was a half-demon? Could he have told anyone else? Had she introduced him to anyone?

We were going through this when I heard footsteps in the hall. Light ones, barely noticeable, but part of me had been listening for them since I sat down.

They stopped outside the meeting room. I turned my chair, as if getting comfortable, and carefully slid my gaze to the partly open door. Lucas peeked around it, finger to his lips, then motioned me out before withdrawing silently.

I waited for a suitable break in Ava's narrative, then excused myself to "ask Savannah to compile a file on fight clubs."

Lucas was in the hall, waiting. Silently, he backed up to the stock room and slipped inside. I was barely through the door before he caught me up in a breath-stopping kiss.

I threw my arms around his neck and kissed him back, reveling in the familiar tug of his hands entwined in my hair, the taste of breath mints hastily chewed on his way up the stairs, the faint citrus scent of his shaving lotion. Whatever problems I had with my husband, they weren't problems *with* my husband. They were the issues that came with his world and the life he'd been thrust into. I was as crazy in love with the guy himself as I'd been when I married him.

When he began unbuttoning my blouse, though, I pulled back. "Client."

"Call Savannah." Lucas flicked open the top button. "She'll cover for you."

"Normally, yes, but this is a teleporting half-demon. A very impatient one who's liable to jump in here any second now."

"We'll move to our office, then." He popped the front clasp on my bra. "It's warded."

"And involves sneaking past the open door of the meeting room."

He cupped my breasts. "You're arguing, but you're not stopping me."

"I'm enjoying it while I can. But maybe, there's enough time to make *you* a little more presentable." I pressed my hand to his crotch, then lowered myself to my knees. "You know I have a thing for storage rooms."

He chuckled. I unzipped his pants.

"Where'd she go?" Ava's voice rang down the hall. "Is that Lucas's suitcase? Is he here?"

I sighed and zipped his pants as I rose.

"If he's here, I want to talk to him," Ava continued.

I opened the door and stepped out. Lucas followed. Savannah walked up behind Ava, who stared at us, nose crinkling.

"What were you doing in there?" Ava said.

"Duh," Savannah muttered. She passed me a file. "The information on fight clubs you asked for, boss." The meeting room was wired to her office and she eavesdropped at will. "Did you find a box of toner in there or are we out?"

"Out."

"Told ya."

While we'd been talking, Ava had managed to zip between Lucas and me, so fast she seemed to have teleported.

"Ava Cookson, sir. So pleased to meet you."

She stared up at him with the kind of adoration usually reserved for rock stars. Behind me, Savannah snickered, and I had to admit, it looked very odd. I love my husband dearly, but he's no rock star. The word most often used to describe Lucas is "geek," which I happen to think is completely unfair.

Lucas is comfortable with the term, though. He even propagates the image, refusing to wear contacts or more flattering suits, keeping his dark hair in a short, nondescript style any barber can manage. He likes to be unassuming, invisible even. While Ava gazed up at him in adoration, he inched backward, gaze sliding to Savannah and me, as if begging for rescue.

"I was just taking Ava's case history," I said. "If you'd care to join us..."

"Oh, we don't need you." Ava waved me away, her eyes never leaving Lucas. "He can take it from here."

Lucas protested. When she insisted, he became visibly annoyed, which for Lucas meant she was seriously pissing him off.

Finally, I said, "Actually, that's probably best. You can handle it, Lucas. I'll start a file."

Lucas asked Ava to excuse us. Savannah practically had to drag her away, but finally they went into the meeting room.

"She's a twit," I said. "And she's got a serious crusader-crush on you. But I think you can handle it."

Spots of color warmed his cheeks. "Of course I can. It's not that. It's—"

"—that you don't like her insulting me. I get that. But you arguing that I'm important doesn't make me important." I lifted onto my tiptoes and kissed his chin. "All things considered, I'm just as happy not dealing with her. I'll listen in on Savannah's line and, when she's gone, we can go look for more toner. I'm sure there's a box in there somewhere."

He gave me a long, delicious kiss that promised a very good night to come, and when we parted and I thought I caught a touch of sadness in his eyes, I told myself I was imagining it. I had to be. Everything was fine. Well, *we* were fine, and that was all that mattered.

Crusader-Crush

I found both Adam and Savannah listening to Lucas and Ava from Savannah's desk. They didn't try to hide it. If Savannah wanted to listen in, she did. Adam wouldn't eavesdrop on his own, but if Savannah did, and the case sounded interesting, he'd be there, too.

Lucas and I didn't care. If we did, we'd say so, and they'd stop. With such a small office, confidentiality just means we don't discuss cases with outsiders. Having Savannah and Adam listen to intake sessions just saves us explaining the case later.

We moved into the office I share with Lucas, where the meeting could be broadcast louder on my speakerphone. As I listened, I sat at my desk, and reviewed Ava's file. Adam stretched out on the divan, jotting notes and exchanging quips and observations with Savannah as she paced.

Ava insisted on retelling her whole story to Lucas. This recital was a lot more emotional. When she spoke of her brother, I could imagine her dabbing moist eyes. When she spoke of his disappearance, she choked up. Yet even in her grief, she managed to flirt outrageously.

She gushed about Lucas's reputation. Simpered about how honored she'd be if he took her case. Added a few extra heartfelt sobs in hopes that he'd come over and comfort her. He didn't, of course. His comfort was offered with words, and even those sounding stilted and formal. Polite and sympathetic, but distant. Which only made her try all the harder.

"Sounds like someone is hoping to pay her bill with an exchange of services," Adam said.

Savannah snorted. "Her ego will take a beating if she tries."

They laughed. I didn't. It was insulting, having a woman throw herself at my husband when she knew I was in the next room.

"So it seems we have two avenues of investigation," Adam said. "The gambling debt and the fight club. I'll take the fight club and—"

"Excuse me?" Savannah strode over. "No offense, fire-boy, but you're a one-trick pony. I'm a dual-purpose, ultra-charged spellcaster."

"And an attractive young woman, which they like," Adam said. "That's why I was about to suggest you come with me."

"Sorry." She lifted his legs from the divan, sat down and let them fall across her lap.

As they bantered, I kept my gaze on my notes. Savannah has had a crush on Adam from the day they met, which wouldn't be so bad, if she hadn't been twelve at the time and he'd been twenty-three. If Adam had noticed, he'd given no sign of it, treating her like a little sister. I'd figured she'd grow out of it, and if she was going to have a teenage crush, Adam was as safe a bet as I could want—someone who'd treat her well, and leave her with a good impression of guys in general.

Except, well, maybe the impression Adam left was *too* good, one no boy her own age could live up to. At twenty-one, her infatuation has mellowed into a solid friendship, but I know she hopes more will come of it. As for Adam, if you'd asked me his feelings a year ago, I'd have said it was strictly friendship. Lately, though, I've caught hints that maybe something's changed, something he isn't quite aware of himself.

I don't have a problem with the age difference. Maturity-wise, Adam has always been on a slow curve. There's a part of me that wants to give things a push. But I know better. They'll have to figure this out for themselves, and it may take a while.

ONCE LUCAS HAD everything he needed, he extricated himself from the meeting. Savannah was chomping at the bit to rescue him, but that would only make things worse, letting Ava think Lucas hadn't ended their meeting of his own free will.

It didn't help that he refused to commit to take her case. Eventually, he got her out of the building and joined us in our office, where I met him with a double-shot of espresso.

"Thank you," he said.

"We still need toner," Savannah said. "Unless that meeting wore you out."

A faint smile. "No, but I think Ava Cookson was enough work for everyone today. I declare the work day officially over."

"Is that a hint?" Savannah said.

"It is."

"Grab your coat, Adam." She stopped beside me. "We're going for drinks, then a movie, so I'll be home late. Don't wait up."

"You buying?" Adam said.

"We'll expense it."

They left. Lucas sipped his espresso until the stairwell door alarm clicked on, then he downed the rest and crossed to my chair.

Divvying up Duties

y the time we actually left the office, it was past six. We grabbed takeout and headed back to the house. Normally, I'd cook dinner, but after three days away, I couldn't trust there'd be anything left in the fridge.

We hadn't discussed Ava's case yet. It could wait, and we were enjoying some quiet time together. It didn't take long before conversation turned to another aspect of work. My Cabal visit. I gave him a rundown, focusing on the reason for his abrupt summons to Miami: a diplomatic situation.

A French Cabal—the Moreaus—had accused the Cortezes of poaching a shaman employee. Not true. The shaman had come to the Cortezes for a job and failed to disclose the fact he was already employed by the Moreau Cabal. When confronted, he claimed the Moreaus had blackmailed him into working for them, and he had proof.

In the past, Benicio would have returned the shaman to the Moreaus to avoid straining international relationships. But now he had to prove to Lucas that the Cortez Cabal could become the kind of organization he'd be comfortable leading, and that didn't include handing over innocent supernaturals to be imprisoned and possibly killed.

"My advice was to negotiate with the Moreaus," I said. "Give them an choice. Take the shaman back on a one-year contract, promising no mistreatment. Or give him to the Cortezes and accept a finder's fee for training him."

"Good idea," Lucas said after finishing a bite of salmon. "Excellent, actually. I'd have been inclined to confront them with proof of blackmail and force them to drop the matter. Your solution is far more elegant."

"Thank you."

"My father agreed, I presume."

"He did."

He speared a baby potato, gaze on his plate. "And he had the backing of the board?"

When I didn't answer, Lucas's shoulders drooped. A faint reaction, but noticeable, like the lines beside his mouth that seemed to deepen every time this happened.

"Who argued it?"

"Carlos. Or, I should say, several of the VPs disagreed and subtly conveyed their opinion to Carlos, who voiced it."

"I suppose I should be glad he's showing up for meetings."

"And showing up sober."

Lucas tried for a smile. The fact was, he'd be a whole lot happier if Carlos did still show up drunk or high. At least then he wouldn't be a threat. But on his brothers' deaths, Carlos had seen an opportunity to seize his birthright, which to him meant seizing all the power—and money—he could. Unfortunately, he was finding supporters in everyone who opposed Lucas and was pleased to have a straw man they could put forward in his place.

We ate in silence for a few minutes, then Lucas said, "I know those meetings couldn't have been easy. Do you want to talk about it?"

"I survived."

"Naturally, but I really think we should talk—"

"Tell me about your trip."

When he hesitated, I thought I saw that sadness flash in his eyes again. Frustration, I decided. He didn't like the situation, and having me dwell on it wasn't going to help.

"Please," I said.

Another hesitation, then he nodded. "The trial went well. Nothing unexpected, although there was a minor glitch when the client's nerve wore thin and he began thinking perhaps he should admit to having set the fire, albeit accidentally..."

WE HAD A good night. Didn't get much sleep, but it wouldn't have been nearly so good a night if we had.

We got to work at nine, late for us. Lucas caught a ride in with me, which is rare—he usually rides his motorcycle, knowing one or both of us will be zipping off at some point during the day and two vehicles would likely be needed. We used to do most of the legwork together, but lately, well, lately it just seems more efficient to divide our resources.

Savannah drove in separately—on *her* bike. She has no excuse, spending most of her time in the office, but she likes her independence. In some things, at least.

I'd texted Adam to say there would be a meeting at nine, and we met up with him and Savannah in the stairwell.

"So we're taking the Cookson case?" Adam said. "Time to divvy up duties?"

"It is," I said as we moved into the meeting room. "We have two avenues to investigate—"

"I called dibs on the fight club." He glanced at Savannah. "Sorry, *we* did."

Lucas took a seat. "Actually, Paige and I are going to take that angle."

Savannah sputtered a laugh. "Yeah, I know you can fight, Lucas. But seriously? Those guys will make you the minute you show up."

Adam nodded. "According to the files, this club is notoriously anti-Cabal."

"I planned to effect a disguise, naturally."

"It won't be enough," Adam said. "They're so worried about Cabal interference they probably have your photo tacked up in the office. And don't tell me you're going to stay in the background and let Paige fight because…" He looked at me, and the corners of his mouth twitched. "Um, no. Just no."

"Thanks." He was right. I could defend myself, but I was no fighter.

"Perhaps you have a point," Lucas said. "But if you've read those files, then you know there are a few types of supernaturals they really don't like in a ring. One is Exustio half-demons. An energy bolt spell is one thing; your powers inflict third-degree burns. As soon as they realized what you are, they'd throw you out."

"Leaving one option for your fighter," Savannah said.

I glanced at Lucas, who nodded, reluctantly.

"Yes, it'll have to be you, Savannah," I said. "But if Ava's right and they like young women, having you show up with Adam will limit your potential. I should play manager."

"I'll accompany you and stay in the background," Lucas said.

"Leaving Adam to check out the gambling lead and no one in the office?"

"I'll take the gambling angle and Lucas can play secretary." Adam caught our looks and sighed. "Or Lucas can follow the lead while I sit on my ass and look pretty."

"Because you're so good at it," Savannah said.

Adam sighed again.

Lucas didn't seem thrilled by the division of duties. To be honest, I was surprised he'd suggested taking the fight club lead himself—he knew he couldn't slip around the supernatural world as easily as he could five years ago. And accompanying Savannah and me? That made no sense at all.

Maybe he'd foreseen the next turn of events. Ava insisted on going with Lucas. When she'd been in San Francisco with her brother, she'd met his debtors. She couldn't describe them or tell us where Jared met them, but she could take Lucas there and point them out.

So he was stuck with her. Annoying, but no reason to pawn her off on Adam and leave the office unmanned while he tagged along with Savannah and me. If I didn't know Lucas better, I'd almost think he was actually worried about spending time with Ava Cookson.

The First Rule of Fight Club

We flew to San Francisco, then rented a car and drove to Santa Cruz. On the way, I read over everything Savannah had compiled on fight clubs.

Unlike the movie, the first rule of our fight clubs was not "don't talk about it." Most supernaturals plugged into the seamier side of our world knew about them. Even finding one wasn't all that tough, if you knew who to ask. Our records named organizers in over a dozen cities. Find them and, theoretically, you'd find a fight club. In the case of the Santa Cruz one, the owners had been running it in the same location for years.

While Adam was right that fight clubs were anti-Cabal, again, the truth wasn't so simple. While outwardly they professed independence of Cabals, our records showed that about half were underwritten by a Cabal. That didn't include the Santa Cruz one, which *was* known to shun all Cabal overtures.

A supernatural fight club is exactly what it sounds like. Supernaturals—usually young, usually male—work off pent-up frustration and energy by fighting. People bet on the outcome.

If there are rules to our fight clubs, the first would be "don't permanently maim or mutilate or murder your opponent." Our files hinted at underground clubs where anything went, but most were very strict about the rule. They had to be. No kid would get into the ring knowing he could be up against a werewolf capable of snapping his neck with a single twist.

Inflict serious damage and the fight would be called at your forfeit. Kill your opponent—even accidentally—and you'd be banned from every fight club for life. Too many deaths could kill a club, so the owners didn't take any chances.

THE ADDRESS IN our files led us to a house in the country. An abandoned house that was past ready to be condemned, every window and door gone, the roof collapsing, the house listing to one side. The surrounding field was so overgrown I wasn't even sure we could *get* to the house.

Savannah idled the car on the road as we looked around. "Looks about right."

"Have some experience with these places?"

"No, but if I was running an illegal supernatural fight club, this is where I'd put it."

"It doesn't look like there's a neighbor in sight, but wouldn't someone notice if there were cars lined up and down this road? If there's a parking lot, I sure don't see—"

She swung the rental car toward the ditch. The tires found a pair of ruts that led past the wire fence and behind a thick patch of trees. There the lane opened into a lot surrounded by grass higher than my head. A vintage Mercedes and a gleaming new pickup were parked at the far side.

"Great, we found the right place," I said. "Now let's get out of here before—"

"No one's around," she said as she finished casting a sensing spell. She got out of the car, walked over to the vehicles and peered inside.

We might have found the club, but Savannah couldn't just walk in and say, "I want to fight." It was invitation only. Ava had provided us with the name of the half-demon friend who'd wrangled her invitation, and said he'd be happy to give one to us, too, but we had to be a little more discreet than that.

I rolled down the window. "We'll come back tonight and scout around. In the meantime, we'll run those license plates and—"

Savannah strode toward a path leading from the lot.

"Hey!" I whispered, as loudly as I dared. "Don't—"

She disappeared into the long grass.

By the time I caught up with Savannah, she was heading toward a barn that looked as rundown as the house. I picked up my pace and joined Savannah as she passed through a small door.

Once inside, I heard the *twackity-thwack-thwack* of someone hitting a boxer's speed bag. We were in a small room with a coat rack and a sign warning that the management wasn't responsible for stolen articles. Underneath, someone had written—"I'm not either" and signed it "Rico." The bouncer, I guessed. Fortunately, he wasn't around now.

From there, we walked though a second door and straight into the fight club. It wasn't a state-of-the-art gym cleverly disguised as a crumbling barn. If it was, I'd have known the Cabals were involved. Still, the place was a lot nicer than you'd expect from the outside.

A professional boxing ring dominated the large, open area. Bleachers stretched along two sides. The third was an empty space for bystanders, with a betting window to the rear. The fourth side was the staging area, where a guy in his early thirties was pummeling a speed bag, dancing in place, sweat dripping down his bare back, wavy dark hair plastered to his forehead and neck.

Savannah paused to admire the view while my gaze moved on to a second man, tapping away on a laptop just inside a tiny office at the back. He was also dark-haired, bearing a strong resemblance to the fighter, but his hair was military short, his physique hidden under a golf shirt and pressed trousers.

The fighter ducked to avoid a hard swing-back, and caught sight of us. He said something to the other man, who rose, frowned and stepped out of his office.

"May I help you?" he said.

"I hope so," Savannah said, mimicking my Boston accent. "I want to fight at your club. Only thing I'm missing is the invitation."

The man's frown deepened. He was older than the boxer by at least a few years, and looked like he'd be more at home in a corporate office. I was going to hazard a guess at his name. Ethan Gallante, club owner along with his brother, Tommy—the speed-bag boxer.

"This isn't how it's done," Ethan said.

I stepped forward. "I know, but Georgia here is new to the circuit. We knew where you were, but don't have any contacts to get an invitation from. Our only other option was to hang around the parking lot tonight, find a gullible-looking guy and convince him to invite us."

"Which could be fun," Savannah said. "But I thought you'd rather we didn't stalk your patrons." She flashed a smile. "And I was really hoping to start fighting tonight."

Ethan walked over and circled her. It was a cool appraisal. Not rude, just disinterested in anything but her potential as a fighter. Tommy was the one giving her a more personal once-over, grinning as if he liked what he saw. Most men do. Savannah looks like she belongs on a runway. Six feet tall, long-legged and willowy with straight dark hair that stretches to the middle of her back and huge eyes so blue she's often accused of wearing color contacts. Her features are strong, severe even, but it only makes her more arresting, paired with those innocent, wide blue eyes.

Savannah looks strong and forceful, direct and confident and men like that...until they realize that the packaging promotes the product accurately. I'd never tell her to tone it down, though. She just needs to find a partner who's confident enough in himself to accept and appreciate her. Like Adam.

The once-over Ethan gave Savannah was more critical than the ones she usually got from men. I could tell he approved of her height, but the rest of the package was a little too fashionable.

"How much fighting experience do you have?" he asked. "Real fighting, without your powers."

"I don't go looking for bar brawls, but I can hold my own."

His expression said he doubted it. "Well, Georgia, I'd love to give you a chance to test that, but I don't see a gym bag, and that outfit definitely isn't—"

Savannah unbuttoned her blouse and tossed it aside, revealing a sports tank in place of a bra. Then she kicked her boots aside and peeled off her jeans. Underneath, she wore spandex exercise shorts.

Ethan took a closer look now. Savannah was in excellent shape. She worked out with Adam, and they were into every outdoor sport imaginable.

"All right, then." He pointed to the ring. "Tommy will give you a few rounds. Save your supernatural powers for an audience. This is strictly hand-to-hand combat."

Tommy grinned. "Which keeps the playing field level for me."

I knew from my files that the Gallantes were a family of necromancers. Unlike witches and sorcerers, necromancy powers hit only a few members every generation. Ethan had them; Tommy didn't.

Tommy and Savannah went into the ring. It was more a test than a fight. Tommy was clearly a pro and he didn't want to show her up, just put her through her paces, see whether she could throw a punch and block one.

When they finished, Tommy congratulated her. Ethan only eyed her for another minute, then said, "Do I know you from somewhere, Georgia?"

"Not unless you hang out at Harvard," she said.

"You look familiar," Ethan said. "But I don't think we've ever met. A relative maybe."

Without waiting for an answer, he walked over to his laptop, typed something in, then said, "You're on the list. Doors open at ten. You'll fight your first round at eleven."

Round One

When we returned at ten-thirty, the small parking lot was already filled, with a young man directing cars to a second one. Although it was just as well hidden, I suspected people living along the road couldn't help but notice the increased traffic. I suppose as long as the brothers kept things quiet, they were willing to look the other way.

And the Gallantes did keep things quiet. Two more young men in the yard directed patrons, making sure they quickly got into the barn. While the brothers hadn't spent a fortune on the gym, they'd obviously splurged on soundproofing. I could barely hear a murmur as we approached the barn.

When we stepped into the bouncer's room and gave our names to Rico, I could make out cheers and boos from within, along with the occasional dull thump of fist hitting flesh. But it wasn't until we opened the inner door that the full cacophony hit us, the cheers becoming shouts, grunts and groans punctuating the thump of the blows.

There were two fighters in the ring. Both were young men. That went for most of the combatants milling around the staging area. The clientele was older, averaging fifty, mostly male. All the women seemed to be attached to a man, and while a few avidly watched the match, more were avidly checking their watches.

Heads turned when we walked in. Then more heads, as people nudged their neighbors. Patrons leaned over to ask Ethan who we were, while the fighters asked Tommy in the staging area. Their gazes swung to Savannah as the brothers presumably said she was fighting tonight. After they checked Savannah out, they asked another question—*who* was she fighting? When they got the answer, they streamed to the betting window.

"Now that's a rousing show of support," Savannah said. "One look at me, and they're slapping down their life savings."

When I didn't answer, she rolled her eyes. "I know they aren't betting on *me*."

She'd made sure of that when she picked her outfit. It was still the same white blouse and chocolate-brown pants from earlier, but she'd bumped up the accessories—chunky necklace, bangle bracelets and gold chain belt, plus boots with stiletto heels. She was better dressed than any of the girlfriends and wives here…and looked even less likely to step into the ring.

We were wandering around, scoping out the place, when another woman walked in, unaccompanied. She was about twenty-five, short and stocky, her broad face set in a permanent "don't fuck with me" scowl.

"I do believe the competition has arrived," Savannah said. "As for supernatural type, I'm betting dwarf." She caught my look. "Yes, I know there's no such thing."

"Not what I was going to say."

She sighed. "Fine, I'll be kind. Short people have their uses." She set her water bottle on my head. "They make great tables. Good footstools, too, once you knock them down, which is exactly what I plan to do with that one."

"Don't get cocky."

The other fighter walked to Ethan and said something to him. He waved Savannah over.

"Georgia? I'd like you to meet Mel. Mel, Georgia. Your opponent tonight."

Savannah extended a hand. Ignoring it, Mel looked Savannah up and down, then turned to Ethan.

"You're kidding, right?"

"Don't worry," Savannah said. "I can fight on my knees."

"I bet you can do a lot on your knees."

"Oooh, trash-talking already! This is going to be so cool!"

"Who's that?" Mel said, gesturing at me. "Your girlfriend?"

"Manager. I'm one-hundred-percent hetero." Savannah bent down to Mel and mock-whispered. "Sorry. You are kinda cute, though."

Mel grabbed Ethan's arm and marched him off. "I thought we talked about this. I want real opponents, not pretty girls…"

Savannah watched her go. "I know, I know. Don't get cocky. She's obviously not an amateur."

"Correct. Now, let's mingle."

MINGLING WASN'T DIFFICULT. The problem was getting away from the men so Savannah could prep for her match. As she changed, I ignored the two guys hitting on me and concentrated on Mel, who was warming up in the staging area. That warm-up included hand exercises and a lot of muttering under her breath. When Savannah emerged, I excused myself from the men and hurried over.

"I know her supernatural type," I said.

"Witch. I know. I asked the guy getting changed next to me, who was distracted enough to forget he's not supposed to tell a new fighter. Any last-minute lectures?"

I shook my head.

Her eyes widened in exaggerated surprise. "Seriously?"

"I could tell you to be careful, but you'd only roll your eyes and say you aren't stupid. I could tell you to not overdo it, but you already know that. I could give you a dozen strategies, but you'd ignore them and do it your way. So all I can say is good luck."

She gave me a one-armed hug. "Thanks." She bent to my ear. "And I will be careful. Not that you're worried or anything."

I was, and she knew it. I also knew better than to show it. I'm not her mother. That's always seemed too strange a role to take when I'm only ten years older. It also seemed disrespectful to her real mother, Eve, who's still around, in spirit if not in body. I see myself more as a big sister. Like a big sister, I can worry, but I'm not supposed to show it too much.

I had reason to worry, too. Even at twenty-one, Savannah is a more powerful spellcaster than Lucas or I can ever hope to be. Her mother was a dark witch and her father was a sorcerer, making her equally proficient at both kinds of magic. Eve was also the daughter of a lord demon, and while Savannah didn't inherit any of those abilities, the demon blood acted as a power boost for a girl who really didn't need it.

When Savannah walked into the staging area, every guy turned to look at her—even the one practice boxing with Mel, who snapped off a left hook to his jaw for it. Mel gave Savannah another once-over, slower now, but ending with the same dismissive sniff. She'd made up her mind about her opponent. If Savannah was in decent physical condition, it was only from too many hours on a treadmill at some overpriced health club. That wouldn't help her in the ring.

I hadn't been watching the match in progress, but I think one of the fighters caught a glimpse of Savannah and was just as distracted as Mel's partner. The next thing I knew, the ref was calling the match and Tommy was striding over to escort Savannah and Mel into the ring.

The whistle had barely sounded before Mel was on Savannah, hitting her hard and fast, as if determined to make a fool of her with a short match. Savannah dodged and ducked, but didn't throw a single punch, infuriating Mel until she resorted to magic—a knockback spell, then an energy bolt, then another knockback. Savannah easily evaded each before dodging behind Mel. She caught Mel's wrists and held them as the woman twisted and snorted like an enraged bull.

"What?" Savannah said. "I'm only holding your hands. That means you can't cast sorcerer magic. But you're a witch.

Don't need your hands for that." She leaned around Mel. "You do *know* witch magic, don't you?"

With a snarl, Mel pulled free and wheeled on Savannah, fist flying. Before it could land, Savannah nailed her with a right hook that sent her reeling, probably more from surprise than force. She bounced back, fingers rising as the first tentative cheers rang out.

"You really like that knockback, don't you?" Savannah said. "Fine, then. I'll let you have it."

Mel hesitated, fingers raised.

"Go on," Savannah said. "I won't even move. Hit me with your best shot."

The knockback struck Savannah in the shoulder, spinning her into the ropes.

"You call that a knockback?" she said as Mel ran at her. "*This* is a knockback."

Savannah hit her with one that hurtled her against the ropes. The tentative cheers turned to a collective whoop.

Mel scowl at the audience, then barreled down on Savannah. Halfway there, she stopped dead, frozen in place.

"Binding spell." Savannah glanced at Ethan. "I suppose that's illegal?"

Ethan looked over at his brother—it was a fighting call, not an administrative one. Tommy just shrugged helplessly.

"Don't get many witches in here, do you?" Savannah said. "Not ones who know their own magic well enough to cast a binding spell, at least. Still, I'd make it illegal. Otherwise, I could just run over and knock her down, which would be terribly unfair."

She released the spell. Caught off guard, Mel toppled. Savannah launched a fireball, whipping it toward Mel's head, making the other woman shriek and duck.

"Damn," Savannah said. "She screams like a girl. Who'd have thought? Witch magic again. Fireball. Minor burns only— no worse than an energy bolt, which is legal. Well, unless you cast them like this."

Savannah whipped an energy bolt at her opponent. It hit the top rope and snapped it, both ends sizzling and jumping like a live wire, onlookers scrambling out of the way.

"Deadly," Savannah said. "Which is why I'll stick to the basic version."

She turned on Mel, who gamely leapt up, fingers out to cast an energy bolt of her own.

"Knockback," Savannah said.

Her cast sent Mel to the mat.

"Fireball."

Savannah singed the ends of Mel's spiky hair, then sent the fireball whipping around her, locking her in place as effectively as any binding spell.

"Minor energy bolt."

Sparks flew from her fingers, and hit Mel like an electric shock.

"And, just because it makes a cool special effect: fog."

She enveloped Mel in silvery mist, but her lips kept moving, and from within the fog, Mel gave an agonized shriek. She crawled out, coughing and sputtering, then collapsed on the mat.

Savannah won.

Black Magic Woman

*A*s Savannah retreated to her corner, I whispered. "What did you use?"

"Energy bolt," she said.

"After that, I mean. The last spell."

"Fog?" When I shook my head, she shrugged. "That's the last one I used."

It wasn't. And I knew by looking at her face that I wouldn't get the answer I wanted.

Savannah has a secret stash of dark magic spells. She thinks Lucas and I don't know about them. We do. We know dark magic is in her blood. We trust her to use the spells with care. But she still won't admit it.

Elena says it's like when Savannah started having sex. She'd lie about spending the night at a friend's place and hide her stash of condoms. Lucas and I knew what she was doing, and we knew she was responsible enough to handle it. The subterfuge made us feel like we hadn't raised her properly, if she thought she had to hide it from us.

I suppose she thought it might change our opinion of her. Or that she'd be subjected to "discussions" she didn't need. I'm not sure using dark magic is quite the same, but I suppose the basic analogy fits. I only hope that someday she'll trust me enough to talk about it.

The main thing was that Mel wasn't seriously injured. Just seriously pissed off. She was still shouting for a rematch when Tommy hustled her out of the gym. No one paid any attention. All eyes were on Savannah as people crowded around, congratulating her, trying to talk to her, trying to set up matches.

She heard none of it. She was on the phone, lost in a call.

A few minutes ago, after taking the towel from me, she'd asked if I'd placed a bet.

"No, but Adam did."

"Betting against me? The bastard."

"Do you seriously think he'd bet *against* you?" I lifted her iPhone. "He even had me record the match, though I don't think we should tell the Gallantes that. Definitely against house rules."

She'd snatched the phone and called him, and left me fielding her congratulations as she laughed and teased and traded quips with Adam. If she did share her dark magic secrets with anyone, it would be him. I hoped she did.

Finally I got her attention and motioned that she needed to get off the phone. We'd come for information and now that she was the center of attention, we needed to take advantage of it.

COUNTERFEIT MAGIC

"Witch versus sorcerer," the balding man was saying. "The match of the century."

Actually, the match of the past *few* centuries, and a rivalry I'd be happy to see die a quiet death. The man continued expounding on his idea for setting Savannah up in a special event. Ethan was listening, but I could see he wasn't interested. Too gimmicky for his tastes.

"They'd each use their own magic, of course," the promoter continued. "The ultimate showdown. Prove for once and for all who has the better magic."

"It's not a matter of *better*," I said. "It's different, and if you restrict a witch to her own spells, you're seriously handicapping her in the ring. While we have minor offensive magic, such as the fireball, most of ours is defensive, like that binding spell. If we have to use our own, you'd have a witch fending off a sorcerer, but doing very little damage, which only lends credence to the stereotype of witches."

"Run, little witch-mouse, run," Savannah muttered. "Hide from the big bad sorcerer."

Ethan nodded. He got it, but the promoter looked as if he'd tuned out halfway through my explanation.

"If you *were* to have a witch versus sorcerer match," I continued, "it would make more sense to let them use any magic they know."

Savannah grinned. "Which would benefit the witch. Most of us learn sorcerer magic, too. Sorcerers don't bother with ours. If that puts them at a disadvantage, it's their own fault. Not like they *can't* learn it."

They continued talking. The conversation wasn't going anywhere useful—not for our investigation's purposes, anyway. I looked around for Tommy and spotted the fighter in the back corner. A man was clearly trying to talk to him, but Tommy didn't want to listen, shaking his head, arms crossed, gaze traveling the room.

I backed up a little for a better look at the situation. The other man was in his fifties. Heavyset. A former fighter? A badly set nose said yes. The cut of his suit, though, insisted he was no has-been. Another promoter? An agent?

Whatever he was trying to tell Tommy, he really wanted to say it, gesturing and leaning forward. The younger man just leaned back and kept shaking his head. Then Tommy went still. He turned to the old fighter, giving him his full attention.

The man said something. Tommy's gaze flitted around the room and landed on his brother. He put a hand on the older man's upper arm, guided him into the office, and shut the door behind them.

I was about to excuse myself from the conversation—and see if I could overhear Tommy's—when the next match was announced. Both were return fighters, so their supernatural types weren't a secret. When they announced that one was a teleporting half-demon, I stopped.

My gaze slid to the office. As interesting as that conversation looked, it was unlikely to have anything to do with Jared Cookson. Better to take advantage of this segue.

I turned to Savannah. "Did you hear that? An Evanidus? That must be tough to beat."

"Hell, yeah," she said. "He can just zip away every time his opponent throws a punch. I'm surprised you allow them, Ethan. Is it even possible to beat one?"

The promoter chuckled. "Oh, yeah, it's possible." He nudged Ethan. "Remember that girl a few months ago?"

Ethan shook his head.

"You should have seen her," the promoter said. "Only a Tripudio, but still able to teleport far enough to avoid a blow. Really pretty girl. All dressed up nice, like you were. Only with her, it wasn't a show."

"Never done more than bitch-slap another girl?" Savannah said.

"I doubt she'd even done that."

"Why would a chick like that even bother showing up?"

Ethan shrugged. "With her powers, I suppose she thought it would be easy money."

The promoter laughed. "Easy money for everyone who bet *against* her. Even the guy she came with did."

"Huh," I said. "Sounds like maybe she threw the fight."

I glanced at Ethan, but his expression was blank—intentionally blank, I suspected.

"I bet she did," Savannah said. "How'd she react when she found out her friend bet against her? No, let me guess. She was furious. Stormed out. Put on a helluva show."

"You got it." The promoter nodded sagely, as if he'd known it was an act, but I could tell the possibility hadn't occurred to him.

Ethan gave no reaction. This wasn't a revelation to him. Spend any amount of time around Ethan Gallante, and you couldn't mistake him for a dumb hustler, easily conned.

It would have looked as if Ava had cheated. Then she roared off in her partner's car, leaving him stranded with the club owners. He wasn't seen again…until his body washed up on the nearby shore.

According to our file, the Gallantes had a reputation for running a fair operation. How far would they go to protect it?

"—how you have to do it," the promoter was saying. He was pointing at the ring, where the Evanidus half-demon was using his power not only to escape blows, but to land them.

Savannah nodded. "If you're a good fighter already, it's a useful power. Otherwise, you're just going to wear yourself out dodging blows."

The half-demon's opponent—a sorcerer—hit him with a knockback. The half-demon staggered against the ropes.

"The sorcerer isn't trying to hide his hand gestures," Savannah said. "He's telegraphing his moves. The half-demon should have been able to zip out of the way easily."

"He should have," the promoter said. "Now watch."

The half-demon righted himself, shaking it off, dazed. The sorcerer smiled, lifted his fingers for a stronger spell—and got grabbed in a head-lock as the half-demon teleported behind him.

The promoter shook his head. "How many times has Davy used that move?"

"Often enough that Leo's an idiot for not seeing it coming," Ethan said as the referee counted down.

The match ended. The half-demon—Davy—left the ring, grinning and accepting high-fives as he went. He headed toward Tommy, and I realized I'd been so caught up in the fight that I hadn't seen Tommy leave the office, which meant I hadn't seen his expression when he did. Now he was grinning at Davy, and the guy who'd taken him aside was nowhere to be seen. Damn.

"Now, Davy would make a good match-up for you, Georgia," Ethan murmured. "Some of our boys would be an ass about fighting a woman, but Davy's a good guy." He paused. "Or perhaps we should start you slower and work up to Davy as a main event."

"That might be a good idea," Savannah said. "Little out of my league right now."

Ethan nodded approvingly, as if he'd been testing whether her ego outweighed her common sense. He'd value the latter, and Savannah was adroit enough to realize that.

"Perhaps Tommy, then. He's a better fighter than Davy, but if we let you use your powers, it would be an even match. A good exhibition event. Introduce you to a bigger crowd. Work up some excitement in the circuit." He started toward his brother, and waved for us to follow.

Davy was still pushing through the throng. When he disappeared, Savannah laughed.

"Taking the express route," she said. "Damn, that's a sweet power."

We watched for Davy to reappear beside Tommy. Instead, a cry went up from the crowd. Someone shouted for a doctor.

Ethan raced over. Davy lay face-down on the floor. Someone reached out to turn him over.

"No!" Ethan said. "Don't touch him. His neck may have been injured in the fight."

"Is he breathing?" someone asked.

"Of course," Ethan said. "He's just unconscious."

"He doesn't look like he's—"

"He's fine." Tommy stepped between his brother and the crowd. "Now everyone out. We need to get Dr. Phillips in here. Rico!"

The bouncer appeared from the cloak room.

"Get the boys and clear this place. Have Pete wait in the parking lot for the doctor."

I squeezed in beside Ethan. "I know first aid. I—"

"I'm a paramedic," Ethan said.

As I rose, I took a closer look at Davy. Then the employees from the parking lot swarmed in, shooing everyone out of the gym. When one tried to move me along, I said I needed to find Savannah and ducked away.

I found her cornered by the promoter again. He was still talking up a sorcerer-witch match. If Ethan wasn't interested, he knew another fight club that would be. She tried to shake him. He wasn't budging, and soon we were swept along with the others, out the door and through the field to our rental.

When we reached the lot, Savannah finally brushed off the promoter, taking his card and promising to call and "talk about it."

Even that brief pause was enough to have one of the guards swoop down and bustle us along until we were in our car and lining up to leave the lot.

"Really eager to get us out of here, aren't they?" Savannah said. When I didn't answer, she glanced at me. "And you know why, don't you?"

"I do. That fighter wasn't unconscious. He was dead."

Taking Care of Business

When the line of cars from the fight club turned right toward Santa Cruz, Savannah turned left. She circled back down the next road until we came out on the other side of the club. We parked, then walked through an outcropping of woods.

The secondary lot was empty. Even the primary lot only had three cars in it—the Mercedes and the pickup from earlier, plus a silver BMW.

"Ethan, Tommy and the doctor," Savannah whispered. "They've gotten rid of everyone else. Even the staff."

A crashing in the undergrowth had us launching cover spells. It was a man, tramping through the field to the small lot. He couldn't have been much over forty, but he heaved and puffed like a locomotive, jowls and belly quivering. The doctor, I presumed, and not one who heeded his own advice about healthy living. As he drew closer, I could see the medical bag in one hand and an envelope in the other. He climbed into his car and roared off.

We released our cover spells.

"Paid him off and sent him on his way," Savannah said. "But why call him in at all, if the guy was already dead?"

"Covering their backs. The staff saw the doctor arrive, and if anyone asks the doctor later, he'll say Davy was fine."

"All that to hide one death? It didn't even happen in the ring. No offense, but maybe you're wrong and the guy really is fine."

I waved toward the barn. "One way to find out."

THAT TOP-NOTCH SOUNDPROOFING job really didn't help when we wanted to eavesdrop. They'd locked the door, too. An unlock spell solved that.

We slid in under blur spells. The voices came clear then— Ethan and Tommy, arguing.

"Do you think I *want* to do this?" Ethan was saying. "If you have a better idea, please let me know, because this is a shitty thing to do to a good kid like Davy."

"Maybe it wouldn't be so bad," Tommy said. "If we just…"

"Told the truth?"

"Yeah."

"Admitted we've had two fighters *die* in the last six months? One more who would have died if I didn't keep an epi pen in the back room? We run a clean game here, Tommy. That's always been our goal—*both* of ours—and it's the only reason these kids come to us instead of flocking to the Warners. They get a whiff of this, and we're through."

Silence. Then Tommy sighed. "You're right. I'll take care of it."

"Thank you."

WE NEVER DID find out exactly what "taking care of it" meant, because right after that they started preparing to move Davy's body, and we didn't dare stick around. We hoped to follow them in the car, but they were gone before we made it back to the rental.

We drove to our hotel in silence. I was busy thinking and Savannah didn't interrupt me. As we walked through the hotel parking lot, I turned my cell on and checked for messages.

"How many times did Lucas call?" she said.

"None."

"Seriously? Better check your phone, 'cause I'm pretty sure your battery's dead."

"It isn't."

"Huh." She pushed the door open for me. "Must be busy fending off Ava, then. Probably praying *you'll* call and rescue him."

I smiled. "Probably."

I phoned Lucas from the elevator. It rang through to voice mail. I left a message.

"So, do I get your theory now?" Savannah said as we walked into our room. "Or can I give you mine first?"

I tugged off my shoes and sat on the edge of my bed. "Go for it."

"Okay, so apparently Ava and her brother weren't as discreet as they thought. Big surprise there. The Gallante brothers suspected they'd cheated. After Jared leaves, they go after him, kill him, toss his body in the bay. One guy dies, no big deal. But then a second guy has an allergic reaction or something and almost dies. And now a third guy really *does* die, and the Gallantes realize they're in deep shit—with Davy dead, someone might find out about Jared and link them to his murder. So they need to hide Davy's body."

"One problem. They said the first death was a fighter. That couldn't be Jared."

"Not necessarily. After Jared won some of the money he owed, maybe he figured entering the ring would be an easy way to win the rest. Tommy fights, so obviously they accept challengers without powers. Jared just says he's from a supernatural family, and they let him in."

"Possible..."

"But you doubt it."

I tugged pins from my hair. "First, I don't think Jared would jump into the ring so fast, not when he made easy money from betting. Second, if the Gallantes killed him, it was accidental. Neither strikes me as a cold-blooded murderer. Tommy could have roughed him up to teach him a lesson and he died of his injuries. But that doesn't explain the first fighter's death." I set the pins on the nightstand. "So either you're right about Jared fighting..."

"Or we have two completely separate cases."

WE WERE GETTING ready for bed when Savannah caught me checking my phone.

"You know why he isn't calling, right?"

My stomach did a strange little clench. "No."

She flopped onto the bed. "Maybe I shouldn't tell you. Spoil the surprise." When I gave her a blank look, she sighed. "My God, Paige, you'd think after eight years with the guy you'd have this figured out by now. He's in San Francisco, right? Only an hour away? He's coming over. Probably has a room reserved already, champagne chilling. A nice romantic getaway. Plus an excuse to bolt from Airhead Ava, which is a huge bonus."

"Did he say he was coming?"

"No."

"Did you tell him where we were staying?"

That gave her pause. "Well, no, but…Okay, maybe he isn't coming tonight, but he will tomorrow, after he casually asks about our hotel."

I glanced at my phone.

"For God's sake, Paige. Just call him already. He's probably trapped. You know Lucas. He's not going to tell Ava to get lost so he can phone you back. Give him the excuse."

I nodded and called. On the second ring, someone picked up. Only it wasn't Lucas.

"Lucas Cortez's phone," Ava chirped. "How may I direct your call?"

She sounded drunk. Music boomed in the background. Annoyance darted through me. I felt…I wasn't sure what I felt, but there was an extra snap to my voice when I asked to speak to Lucas. She passed the phone over, giggling as Lucas said something I didn't catch.

"Hello?"

"It's me."

"Paige." He sounded relieved. "Just a moment."

He murmured something to Ava. She twittered that she'd get him a refill. The music receded as he moved to a quieter spot.

"You sound like you're in a bar."

"Hmm."

His tone suggested it wasn't by choice. He went on to say he'd gotten my message and had been trying to get away to return my call before I went to bed.

We talked about the case. He agreed with my theories. His own leads weren't nearly as promising.

"Chasing gambling debts is rather mundane, particularly when they don't seem to be leading anywhere," he said.

"I bet."

There was a pause. Probably looking around, wondering when Ava was going to show up. I waited. After a moment, he cleared his throat and said, "I suppose that any lead should be followed to its end."

"Unfortunately." I remembered what Savannah had said. "And if we don't finish ours tomorrow, I could always swing by there. It's not much of a drive."

"To San Francisco, no. To L.A., yes."

"L.A.?"

"It appears that's where the loan sharks are based. They have a hangout here, which is where Ava met them with Jared, but they're back in Los Angeles now. If I continue on this lead, I'll need to go there tomorrow, which means notifying Sean, so he can let his family know I'm in town."

Sean Nast was Savannah's half-brother and heir to the Nast Cabal, based in Los Angeles. Now that Lucas officially did some work for the Cortezes, he needed to notify other Cabals if he'd be in their territory.

"Travel has gotten a whole lot more complicated, hasn't it?" I said.

"Among other things. So, while I would love to see you tomorrow night, it won't work out."

"Oh."

I let the silence hang. He could come here tonight. There was still time. Just ask where I was staying…I shook off the thought. That was silly. Selfish, too. He had leads to follow and couldn't spend half the night commuting to see me.

We talked a while longer, then I hung up. When I looked over at Savannah, she was watching me. She said nothing until I crawled into bed, then, "Are you guys okay?"

"Sure." I must not have sounded convincing enough because worry clouded her eyes. "We're fine, Savannah."

She watched me for a few more seconds, then turned off the light.

I WAS DISAPPOINTED that Lucas wasn't coming, but I had to be careful around Savannah. Even the hint of trouble between Lucas and me brought out a side of her we didn't see very often. A vulnerable side, a little girl who'd lost her beloved mother and hadn't known her father, then got a second chance at a family with us. No matter how often we'd told her, when she was younger, that our little spats meant nothing—and they certainly *were* nothing compared to the knockdown, blowout fights our friends had—she felt threatened and she got nervous. Even now that she was an adult, that hadn't changed.

But Lucas and I were fine. Just fine.

I rolled onto my stomach, crossed my arms under my chin and stared at the headboard.

We were fine, weren't we?

Yes, my issues with the Cabal were gnawing holes in my self-esteem, but I was being careful not to let that spill into my relationship with Lucas. He was right to help his father with the Cabal. I believed in that and I believed in him, and I wanted to fully support him, which meant keeping my problems to myself.

Whatever external issues I was dealing with, I was fine with Lucas. But what about him? Was he fine with me?

Savannah was right. Sneaking down here for a romantic surprise was just the kind of thing he used to do. Before his brothers died. Before the Cabal moved into our lives.

He would have called, too. Texted me, at least, ostensibly to get updates on the case, but really just to connect. Why hadn't he done that today?

When was the last time he *had* done that?

Had he really been trapped with Ava, unable to return my call? Or had I moved to the bottom of the priority list? Just his wife. He'd call me back when he could. After he was done having a few drinks with a beautiful young blonde with a damsel-in-distress complex.

I silently laughed at the thought. Um, no. Not Lucas.

Still, while I knew no young blonde could tempt him to stray, I could see how the "damsel-in-distress" part might appeal to a deeper need. Lucas liked saving people. That's how we'd met. He'd come to rescue Savannah and me from the Nast Cabal, and found two very unappreciative damsels. As a client, I'd been less than satisfactory. As a lover, I'd been exactly what he wanted—a woman who could look after herself, and was more interested helping him rescue others than in being rescued herself.

And yet, maybe what he needed eight years ago wasn't necessarily what he needed today. Maybe *I* wasn't what he needed today.

So what he needed was a ditzy girl barely older than Savannah? Someone to make him feel big and strong?

I shook my head and thumped my face onto the pillow. Now I was being stupid. And insulting to Lucas. If he felt the need to offset the ethical challenges of working for a Cabal, he'd get his confidence boost through work, not pretty girls.

There was an issue here I'd been ignoring, though. I wasn't the only one uncomfortable with the new semi-alliance with the Cortez Cabal. I wasn't the only one struggling to find a balance. But the fight I focused on was my own.

I was feeling put out because he hadn't planned any romantic interludes in a while? Why did *he* need to plan them? That was incredibly sexist of me.

I crept out of bed, opened my laptop and started exploring a few ideas of my own.

Under
New
Management

The next morning, Savannah fired me as her manager and made an appointment to interview my replacement. I'd be a lot more hurt about that if it hadn't been my idea. Still, I will admit to being a little miffed at how quickly the real ones had swooped down after her match, whispering—in front of me—that she seemed to be in need of better management.

Over breakfast, we went through the half-dozen business cards and compared recollections of those who'd slipped them into her pocket. When we reached the last, I took one look at the name and slapped it onto the table, brushing the others aside.

"This one," I said. "Call it a hunch."

"Right. The day you or Lucas act on a hunch is the day I give up spell-casting." She lifted the card and peered at it. "Travis Nichols. Say, isn't that—"

"The manager of the young man who died last night. Davy."

"Well, he definitely needs a new fighter. He just doesn't realize it yet."

As we headed up to our room after breakfast, I suggested ways I could be in on the interview, without actually being there.

"We should have brought that new spy camera the Cabal tech lab gave Lucas," I said. "I've been dying to try it out."

"Geeks and their tech toys," Savannah said. "Let's keep this simple, shall we? You want to be in on the interview? Come along."

"Right. Help you find a new manager after you fired me."

"I didn't fire you. You quit. Just when my career starts to take off, and I need you more than ever. Ungrateful bitch." She opened the hotel room door. "But just to show there's no hard feelings, I'm going to let you come with me."

"You're too kind."

When Travis Nichols opened the door and saw both of us standing there, he stood there, gaping, then snapped his jaw shut and waved us inside with a smile as phony as his hair-weave.

"Come in, come in. So happy to see you. *Both* of you." He cleared his throat. "Georgia, could I speak to you for a moment? If you'll excuse us, Miss…Sorry, I didn't catch your name."

"Manager," I said. "Ms. Ex Manager."

He stumbled and stammered about misunderstandings, and how he hoped he hadn't stepped on any toes, and he didn't realize Georgia was already represented or he'd never...

"It's okay," I said. "You were right. She needs someone else. Someone with experience."

I followed Savannah into the living room, turning to wave the startled Nichols through as if he was the guest.

I continued, "I'm not a professional manager. Just a friend looking out for Georgia. Now that she's won her first official bout, I'm happy to step aside. But, being a friend, I'm not going to just walk away. I'm here to hear what you have to offer and help her make a decision."

That put him at ease, and he laid out his offer. I had to nudge Savannah a couple of times to remind her to at least appear interested. She was restless, shifting and squirming and trying to hurry his pitch along so we could get to our part.

Finally he finished. I asked him some questions. Savannah didn't. I doubted she'd been paying enough attention to know what to ask. Then, as we relaxed with coffee and slid into the "getting to know you" part of the interview, I asked, "So, were you at the club last night on business? Do you represent one of the fighters?"

"Davy Jones." He laughed. "And, yes, that's his real name, poor kid." His smile faded and he reached for his cell phone, checking it. "I've left him a few messages. That was a bad fall he took last night."

"I saw. What happened?"

"Lousy refereeing, that's what. Believe me, I'm going to have a talk with Ethan about that. Clearly Leo cast one of those knockback spells right at Davy's head, and that's against the rules. He's just lucky my boy didn't get a concussion or I'd have his ass kicked off the circuit."

"Is the refereeing there always so bad?" Savannah asked. "Ethan was talking about setting me up in a match against Tommy, but maybe it's not the best place for me to start a career."

"You against Tommy?" Nichols' dark eyes glittered. "That's gold, girl. Doesn't matter if you win or lose, it'd get your name traveling through the circuit. Tommy's good. Damn good. Too good for…" He stopped, shrugged. "Well, you know."

"He's professionally trained, isn't he?" I said.

"Hell, yeah. State champion in high school, and that's just boxing. He racked up medals in wrestling, too. Everyone expected him to hit the pro circuit after graduating. But Ethan wanted him to go to college. Nothing wrong with that, of course. Ethan only wanted the best for his little brother. He didn't get to finish college himself. Their folks died when he was in his first year, and Tommy was only a kid and…Well, I'm sure you don't want to hear this."

"Actually, we do," I said. "If Georgia's going to fight at the Gallantes' club, I'd appreciate a little background. So Ethan raised Tommy?"

"Right. He sent him off to college. Can't remember what he majored in. Didn't matter, really, because everyone figured he'd graduate and go back to fighting. Only he didn't. Not on the pro circuit, anyway. He got a job working at a gym downtown."

"What happened?" I asked. "Was he injured?"

"No, it's just..." Nichols rubbed his mouth. "Word is, Ethan didn't want him playing pro. He didn't think Tommy had what it took, and didn't want him wasting his time on it."

"Nice brother," Savannah muttered.

"How did Ethan stop him?" I asked.

Nichols shrugged. "Just talked him out of it, I guess. Convinced him he didn't have what it took. I don't know the whole story. That's just the rumor. Anyway, I'm sure Ethan thought it was best for Tommy. Few years later, they opened the club together, and I think that was Ethan's way of making it up to his brother. Tommy sure as hell doesn't bear him any ill will. Those two are as close as ever. Still live in the same house where they grew up."

"Okay," Savannah said. "So obviously with Tommy's rep, getting a fight against him would be a sweet start to my pro career. But if the club is badly managed..."

"Hell, no, it's one of the best around. The ref missed a call. It happens. Even I didn't see Leo cast that knockback or whatever he did. I'll talk to Ethan and, sure, I'll give him shit for it, but that's just me, watching out for my boys, like I always do. Just last year, one of them..."

He launched into an anecdote to prove to Savannah he'd make a good manager. I kept her from interrupting, but as soon as he finished, she said, "So the Gallantes are good? Fair? That's what I've heard, but you never know."

"I run my boys all up and down the fight clubs in this state. Even over to Texas when the money's right. But all other things being equal, you'll find them fighting for Ethan and Tommy. That's my choice and it's theirs, too. Now, some folks will say the Gallantes are too clean to run a fight club. I say bullshit. Those boys have carved out a nice little niche in the market for those who prefer a fair fight to a bloodbath."

"But there's a point where you can be *too* fair, overly cautious," Savannah said. "Like not wanting to call out a cheater in case you're wrong."

"Uh-uh. Believe me, with the Gallantes, fair means no cheating. They catch you, you're banned for life. Lost one of my own boys that way. He was in a slump, started taking some junk, they caught him, and he was out. Out of my stable, too."

"Sure, but what about throwing games? I heard there was an incident just a few months ago, with another teleporting half-demon. They suspect she threw the fight so her friend could cash in. If the Gallantes knew it and they let them go…"

Nichols laughed. "Oh, they didn't let them go. Sure, the girl got away, but she left her friend stranded. And when that boy finally did leave, Tommy followed."

The Art of Blackmail

*M*an, that Ethan's a piece of work," Savannah said when we got into the car. "Can you believe what he did to his brother? Deciding he's not good enough to turn pro? Tommy should have taken *him* into the ring years ago."

I gazed out the window and said nothing. There'd been a time when Savannah had wanted a career as an artist, and while I'd never have denied her the chance to go to art school, part of me had wondered if encouraging her wholeheartedly had been the right thing to do.

Savannah had talent, but no more than thousands of other kids who dreamed of their first gallery opening. We'd subtly tried to steer her toward graphic design or another use for her skills so she could make a living while pursuing art on the side. She hadn't been interested in that. She wanted to be an artist.

In the end, it was Savannah herself who changed her mind. As high school had progressed, her interest in art had waned. These days, it was only a hobby. She'd found her passion in her job. Well, not her actual job as admin assistant. What she loved were these forays into the field that she hoped would get her out of the receptionist's chair for good. And they would, as soon as she'd matured a little more.

If Savannah had been hell-bent on art school, would I have found a way to convince her not to go? No. I couldn't do what Ethan had done. But I'd have been tempted.

I had to admit, though, that it was different with Tommy. Being state champ meant he did have the talent to go pro. He might not have become a star, but he could have made a living at it for a while. Was that what Ethan feared? A short-lived career? Retiring young, bitter and disillusioned, with nothing to fall back on? Had he set Tommy on a different path to spare him that fate? As someone in a similar position—raising a younger "sibling"—I could understand that urge to protect. I just wasn't sure I agreed with it.

Thinking of retired fighters reminded me of the scene I'd witnessed at the ring, Tommy talking to that former boxer. Had the man been trying to lure Tommy into a bigger arena? What had he said that had alarmed Tommy? Made him look over at Ethan and move the conversation to the office?

"Okay, you're thinking something," Savannah said. "What's the plan, boss?"

"We need to speak to the Gallante brothers again. Separately this time."

FINDING AN ADDRESS for the Gallantes was easy enough. Nichols said they'd lived in the same house all their lives. A simple property search gave us a location on the other side of Santa Cruz.

While Savannah drove, I worked on theories. From Nichols, we'd confirmed that Jared hadn't fought in the ring the night he died, which meant that when the Gallantes talked about another fighter's death, they didn't mean him. Which left us with a problem.

I could see Tommy Gallante going after Jared and beating the crap out of him. I'd spent enough time around werewolves to understand that in some subcultures, violence was the language everyone understood. As even-tempered as Tommy seemed, he *was* a fighter.

So Tommy beats up Jared, who accidentally dies. Then they have a fighter who also accidentally dies, another who accidentally almost dies and another who dies last night... again, accidentally.

"Either these guys aren't nearly as clean as they seem," Savannah said. "Or I really hope all their insurance is paid up, because someone's put one hell of a curse spell on them."

WE FOUND THE house—a small, Southwestern-style ranch in an older neighborhood. The Mercedes was under a carport, but there was no sign of the truck.

"Ethan's in; Tommy's out," Savannah said. "Good enough?"

I nodded.

We parked a couple of doors down and were walking toward the house when the front door swung open. I cast a quick cover spell. Savannah did the same.

It was Ethan grabbing the mail, shirt untucked and half-buttoned, feet bare. He stepped halfway out, and propped the door open with his back. Then he stayed there, flipping through the mail with his back to us. I broke my spell and motioned that we'd continue our approach.

We were close enough to call a greeting when Ethan's cell phone rang. He answered, still sorting mail. Then he stopped.

"Who is this?" he said, voice loud and harsh enough to reach us.

We vanished under fresh cover spells.

"Either you give me your name or—" Pause. "Absolutely not. Anything you have to say to me, say it in the next thirty seconds or—" Pause. His shoulders went rigid, then he spat. "Fine," and hung up.

He tossed the mail inside and tucked in his shirt as he stepped in after it. The door didn't even get a chance to close before he was striding out again, shoes and keys in hand. Seconds later, the Mercedes roared from the drive.

"Follow?" Savannah said as she broke her spell.

"Absolutely."

ETHAN WENT STRAIGHT to the club, fast enough that I was glad I'd let Savannah take the wheel. We parked where we had after last night's match, then cut through the wooded field again. Ethan's car was there, alongside an old Camaro, complete with an eagle on the hood and big-breasted women on the mud-flaps.

"Classy," Savannah said. "Love the mud flaps. I didn't think they still made those."

"No hit on the plate," I said as I finished searching it on my phone. "Fake."

"Like I said, a classy guy. Since we don't have a name, I vote for Guido." She caught my look. "Yeah, yeah, I'm sure there are perfectly nice guys named Guido. In some universe."

We made our way inside the barn. Ethan and his guest— no, I wasn't calling him Guido—were in the office. We zipped into the main room under blur spells. In the silence, the voices came clearly through the closed office door.

Ethan was talking. "—listened to what you have to say. Now I'd like you to leave."

"I'm only trying to help," the other man whined.

"No, you're trying to blackmail me. I suspect you're new to it, so let me give you some advice. In order to effect a successful blackmail scheme, you need to know something blackmail worthy. Something important to your victim."

"Important? Your brother is trying to sabotage your operation here and—"

"The second piece of advice? Do your research. Make sure your information is reliable. If you're going to try passing off lies, at least be sure the lie will work. Know who you're dealing with."

"I know who I'm dealing with. A guy who gave up his *life* to look after a kid brother who's now—"

"Turning on him. Ruining the business. After I devoted my life to raising him. After I built this club so he'd have a place to fight. Is this where I start ranting? Swear vengeance? As I said, *sir*, do your research. You've cast me in a very poorly fitting role. You can bring me all the evidence you want; my answer will remain the same. I trust my brother."

"Then you're a fool."

"Perhaps I am. Now, if you'll excuse me, I have work to do."

We zipped out ahead of Ethan and his visitor. The other man left. We followed and got a few pictures of him. Then we went back to the barn.

Ethan was still in his office.

"Hey," Savannah said. "I hope it's okay coming by like this—"

He turned in his chair, the squeak cutting Savannah short.

"Hello, Georgia," he said. "Or do you prefer Savannah?"

Before I could find my voice, Ethan continued. "You woke me up in the middle of the night, you know. I suddenly remembered where I knew you from. Well, not you. Your mother. I met her once. I was sixteen, just starting to see ghosts. My father had heard that Eve Levine knew a spell that would fix that."

"Fix it?"

"Take away my powers. Or at least make them more manageable. Necromancy drove my grandmother mad. An old story. My father didn't want that for me, so he took me to your mother. Turned out the rumor was false. There is no such spell. She was nice enough about it, considering her reputation. Gave us some vervain to help me banish ghosts and told us where to buy more."

"Since you know my mother's rep, you know why I used a fake name. No one's going into a ring against Eve Levine's daughter."

"True, but that's not the side of the family you're trying to hide. I contacted a few sources this morning. Information is still trickling in, but I did get the identity of your father. Clever of the Nasts, sending a witch as a spy. Please tell your family that if they insist on sending spies and blackmailers, I'll file a complaint with the interracial council. I hear they're actually getting off their asses and doing something about issues like this."

"We're trying," I said.

Ethan turned to me, as if he'd forgotten I was there.

"If you want to complain to the council, that'd be her," Savannah said. "Alternatively, you could hire Lucas Cortez to defend you. That'd also be her. But if you want to send a message to the Nasts, that *wouldn't* be me. I could try, but I think they have special spells on their L.A. office now, just to make sure I don't get past the front door."

I stepped forward and extended my hand. "Paige Winterbourne. I'm—"

"Head of the interracial council," Ethan finished. "And wife to Lucas Cortez."

It'd been a long time since I'd been identified in that order. "Right on both counts. But I'm not here representing the council or the Cabal. I'm investigating the death of Jared Cookson—the young man who bet against his teleporting half-demon sister. Can we talk?"

Brotherly Love

Once we'd settled into chairs in Ethan's tiny office, I explained the situation. As investigative techniques went, this was far from ideal. But he'd thrown us a curve ball with his knowledge of Savannah, and coming clean seemed my only option.

When I finished, Ethan took a moment to gather his thoughts, calmly, seemingly unconcerned that it might make him appear to be concocting a story. As he paused, I looked around the office. A sterile and efficient workspace...with one exception. On a shelf, amidst binders and books, were half a dozen boxing and wrestling trophies.

Tommy's awards, not displayed in the main room as advertising, but here, kept by Ethan. Odd that he'd do that if he'd dissuaded Tommy from a professional career.

"If Jared Cookson is dead, we know nothing about it," Ethan said finally. "Yes, we thought he cheated. Yes, Tommy discussed it with him. And by discussed, I don't mean he took him for a beer and gave him betting advice. Tommy is our enforcer, however uncomfortable he might be in the role. He followed the boy and demanded our money back. Jared resisted. According to Tommy, he didn't resist past a few blows. After getting our money back, Tommy left him walking and talking."

"Or so Tommy said," Savannah said.

"Which means it's the truth. But I don't expect you to believe that, so please feel free to ask him yourself."

"A blow to the head could still do it," I said. "Like that fighter who collapsed last night. Jared walked away, then later he became disoriented from a concussion and ended up in the bay."

Ethan shook his head. "Tommy is very careful about that. No hard blows to the head. An attack designed to scare, not seriously injure."

"Maybe that's his usual way of handling things," Savannah said. "But that's not how this one went down. The kid smart-mouthed Tommy. Or your brother's adrenaline was running high from the club. Things got out of hand."

"Not Tommy."

"You keep saying that. We heard you saying it to that black-mailer, too. Protesting a little much, don't you think?"

Ethan's cool gaze met hers. "Not protesting at all. Simply stating facts."

"That blackmailer accused Tommy of betraying you," I said. "Of trying to shut down the club. He said he had evidence."

"Manufactured evidence."

"You sound damned sure of that," Savannah said.

"I am."

"What did he accuse Tommy of?" I asked.

Now those cool eyes turned my way. "A matter unrelated to this boy's death. A matter that is being taken care of and that, I can assure you, has nothing to do with my brother."

A matter of murder, the death of two fighters. A matter that someone thought was related to Tommy Gallante. I wasn't sure I disagreed.

We tried to get more from Ethan, but the only thing he'd provide was a location for his brother. To be honest, I was surprised he gave that, but I suppose he knew we'd track him down sooner or later, and he didn't want to start trouble with the council.

Tommy was at a gym in Santa Cruz, where he worked part-time, as Ethan did as a paramedic, providing a legitimate source of income for the authorities.

The gym was what I'd expect—shabby but clean, a place for local fighters to train and a place for neighborhood kids to learn the basics.

"And look who teaches the kiddies," Savannah said, rapping her knuckle against a dog-eared poster. It promised free after-school lessons, taught by former state champion Tommy Gallante.

"I bet he does it for free, too." She shook her head. "Some people, huh? Raising a kid who isn't their own. Running a squeaky clean business. Finding time for community work. There's good and then there's too good."

"I'm not sure how good you can be if you're running an illegal gambling operation."

She looked at me. "You're running an illegal gambling operation?"

"I thought we were talking about the Gallantes."

"Oh, right. Damn." She looked over at me. "Do you think we *could* run an illegal gambling operation?"

I pushed her toward the doors. She swung them open and breezed through, and for perhaps the first time since she'd turned sixteen, Savannah walked into a room full of young men and not one glanced her way. That may have had something to do with the drama playing out ringside.

A hulking young man was leaning over the ropes, sweat dripping from his bald head. Behind him, his opponent staggered toward his corner, blood trailing in his wake.

"Now will you fight me, you arrogant son-of-a-bitch?" the bald fighter shouted to someone ringside.

The reply came so softly I barely heard it. "No, and it doesn't matter how many bouts you win, Max, I'm not ever going to fight you."

With a snarl of rage, the fighter leapt over the ropes and flew at his unseen target. Two guys rushed in to the other man's defense, but he only rose from the bench, waving them off. As he did, I saw his face. Tommy Gallante.

Tommy stood his ground as the bald fighter loomed over him.

"I'm not fighting you, Max, and that's not an insult. I'm just not interested."

The fighter grabbed Tommy by the shirtfront.

"Uh-oh," Savannah murmured. "That's not smart."

Tommy didn't throw a punch. He just let the younger fighter put him up against the wall, then calmly said, "Okay, you got me. If you want, you can throw me down and tell everyone you beat me, and I won't argue. Is that what you want, Max?"

"I want you in the ring, Gallante."

"Well, it's not happening. I concede to your superior skills. Now, if you'll excuse me, a couple of pretty girls just walked in, and I really hope they're looking for me."

Max dropped Tommy hard enough to make him stagger. He recovered his balance, then flashed us a big smile and strolled over as if nothing had happened.

"Hey, ladies," he said. "Ethan said you were coming to see me. Paige and Savannah, right?"

"That's right," I said, extending a hand.

We did proper introductions, but I was sure his brother had already told him who we really were and why we were there. He took us into an empty office and ran through his encounter with Jared. He gave more details, but in essence, it matched his brother's story.

"So, you're the club enforcer," Savannah said when he finished. "You like doing that?"

He looked from her to me, then sighed. "Okay, what did Ethan say? No, let me guess. He told you I hate it."

"You don't?"

"Mmm, let's just say it's not my favorite part of the job. But it *is* my job. It's a bit of an ongoing dispute between me and my brother. He knows I don't like it, so he wants to have one of our boys take over. How would that reflect on me as the club's top fighter? I need to play the heavy, even if it's not my favorite role."

"We saw that," I said, nodding toward the ring.

Tommy shifted. "Yeah, well, that's how it goes. You're the lead fighter, everyone wants a piece of you. In the club, we can control it. Here? I don't have time for guys like Max."

"You handled it well," I said. "Not many fighters could step down like that. This sport runs on adrenaline."

"Not adrenaline." He slid off the desk and waved us to the window overlooking the ring. Inside, Max was pummeling another opponent. "You look at his face, what do you see? Adrenaline?"

I watched for a minutes. "No, I see anger. Rage. And that's what you don't have. It's why you're not comfortable being the club's enforcer, and it's why Ethan stopped you from going pro."

Tommy laughed. "Heard that story, have you? My evil older brother squashing my dreams? Yes, he was concerned. Yes, I'm sure he wanted to discourage me. But he never did."

He crossed to a poster on the wall, advertising a bout between him and another former school champion. "*This* is what I'm good at. High school matches, where technique is what counts. When I tried a few pro bouts, I discovered I was missing something most fighters have. Drive."

He sat on the desk again. "Not the drive to win, but the drive to pummel a stranger into hamburger. When a guy fights me in the ring, I'm going to give it everything I've got, then I'm going to ask him out for a beer after. It's just a game to me. Once you hit the pro stage, it's not like that anymore. You're up against guys who are mad at the world, like Max."

"But you still can't escape your reputation," I said. "It's not just other fighters like Max who pester you, is it?" I mentioned the man I'd seen him talking to the night before.

"Promoter. They don't come after me that often anymore, but this guy heard..." He trailed off and shrugged. "Stupid rumor about the club. Nothing to it."

Were people figuring out that the Gallantes seemed a little accident prone?

Savannah missed the cue and barreled forward. "So Ethan didn't make you go to college. But he couldn't resist using you to open a club."

This time, Tommy's laugh boomed through the room. "Using me. Right. That Ethan, it's all about him." He shook his head. "The club was my idea, too. Ethan fully supported it. Even took out a mortgage on our parents' home to set it up. Yeah, maybe there's a little guilt there—he wonders if I chose college to make him happy—but if anyone did the manipulating, it was me." He grinned. "That's the power of being a little brother."

"OKAY, I'VE SOLVED the case," Savannah said as we walked out of the club. "Well, not our case, because I have no idea who killed Jared Cookson, and frankly, I don't care. He sounds like a little snot."

I sighed.

"What? You're thinking the same thing. You just can't say it because that would be wrong. Forget Jared for now. I know who's killing the fighters. The same brother who wants the club shut down. Only it isn't Tommy."

"Ethan?"

"Obviously. Yeah, I know Tommy was teasing about manipulating him, but there's truth there, too. Ethan raises the kid. Maybe expects it to pay off when Tommy goes pro. Only he wimps out and goes to college—"

"That's hardly wimping out."

"Whatever. Point is, Ethan lost his ticket to the high life. Probably got stuck with the tuition bill to boot. Then Tommy guilts him into opening the club. It's more hassle than Ethan wants. He's risking jail time for a business that might barely turn a profit. He's spent twenty years taking care of his brother. The guy hasn't even moved out of the house yet, for God's sake. Now Ethan's had enough. Time to make the club dream go poof."

She rounded the corner, striding to our car and glowering at two school-age kids checking it out. When one reached for the door handle, she zapped him with a small energy bolt. He fell back with a yelp and they took off.

She clicked the fob to open our doors. "People have caught wind of the deaths. First that promoter, then the blackmailer. He has evidence that a brother is involved, and has heard the rumor that Ethan forced Tommy out of the biz so he presumes Tommy's behind it. But who's more likely to have found a way to kill those guys from across the room? The fighter? Or the paramedic?"

I climbed into the car. When I still hadn't said anything and we were pulling from the lot, Savannah glanced over. "You disagree."

"Let's just say I'm not convinced. I think it's a little coincidental that a fighter died last night, when we were there, and that Ethan got a blackmail call just as we're walking toward his house."

"You think Ethan isn't the only one who made us?"

"I think Lucas isn't the only one reaching the stage where he needs to presume most supernaturals know who he is."

Follow the Money

As we headed to the hotel, my phone beeped, reminding me I had a message. It'd come in while we were with Tommy, but I'd forgotten to check afterward. Now I read Lucas's text.

"Well, I'm pretty sure the Gallantes had nothing to do with Jared's death," I said when I finished.

"What?"

I motioned for Savannah to keep driving, then sent back a response and a question. The answer came in seconds.

"Lucas is on his way to L.A., but he just got a call-back from one of Jared's friends. The last time he saw Jared was the day *after* Jared left the fight club."

"Maybe Tommy hadn't found him yet."

"No, he had. Jared was trying to reduce the swelling from a black eye and complaining about a loose tooth."

"So he was fine after the beating. But maybe he went back to the club looking for revenge, and a second beating got him killed."

"Possible. Yet according to the friend, Jared was more frightened than angry. Something—or someone—had him very scared. I think I know what it was."

I started a reply to Lucas.

"Going to share?" Savannah said as I texted.

"Why did Tommy go after Jared?"

"To teach the brat a lesson."

"No. Not really."

As she turned a corner, she checked her mirrors for anyone tailing us. "To get back the money. Which he did. Meaning Jared had nothing left to pay off his debts."

"Exactly."

AT THE HOTEL, I took a good hard look at Ethan and Tommy Gallante, harder than I had earlier, when I thought they were just a step along the path in retracing Jared's final days. I conducted the kind of background check that disputed Savannah's assertion about our squeaky clean business. What we run is an *effective* business and sometimes that takes creative and ethically questionable applications of my computer skills.

"The club is profitable," I said after I'd done my research. "The brothers paid off that mortgage a year after taking it out. Tommy bought his truck last year without taking a loan. The Mercedes is older, but no loans there either. No lines of credit at all. These guys even pay off their cards every month. They aren't multimillionaires, but they certainly aren't in debt."

"Okay, so no financial motivation to shut down the club. Maybe Ethan just wants out. Get his own life. Leave California. Marry, have kids. Only he's tied to his brother through an illegal business. Tommy's not going to let him leave easily. Christ, the guy still lives with him. Imagine how you'll feel if I'm still leaving gobs of toothpaste in your sink a decade from now."

"Tommy hasn't always lived at home. He went to college in Texas."

"Okay, so he moved out for a couple of years—"

"Then came back to Santa Cruz and rented an apartment, where he lived until he got married and bought a condo with his wife."

"Wife?"

"Soon to be ex-wife." I tapped the computer screen. "The divorce is almost final. After they filed, Tommy moved in with Ethan while his wife stayed in the condo. We know Tommy's not a fighter at heart. Ethan probably insisted he move back in until the divorce was done, to avoid putting him through the hassle of bickering over the condo."

"Damn. Blows my theory out of the water. What about the wife, then? Could she be sabotaging the business?"

"If she knew her ex was running an illegal fight club and she wanted revenge, it would be a lot easier just to notify the authorities."

"True. Okay, so if it's not Ethan and it's not Tommy, who the hell is it?"

"I think it's time to ask them that."

THE GALLANTES WEREN'T at the club when we arrived, so we parked down the road and waited. They arrived later in the afternoon. We gave them time to get in and settled, then followed, and found them right where they'd been the day before— Ethan on his laptop and Tommy working out, push-ups this time.

Tommy rose as we entered. "I'm hoping you're here to talk about that bout Ethan suggested. You and me. Make a helluva fight. But I have a feeling that's not it."

Ethan stepped out of his office. "Tommy didn't kill that boy. Neither of us did."

"We're not here to talk about Jared's death," Savannah said. "We're here to talk about Davy's."

I said, "I've seen enough dead bodies to know there's no way, short of necromancy, that Davy Jones walked out of here last night. If you insist otherwise, then I'd like to speak to him. Refuse and I'll get in touch with someone else. Dr. Phillips."

I pulled a chair from the office and sat. "Did you know we have a file on Dr. Phillips? Seems there's a reason he needs that extra cash. His daughter is up on drug charges in Orlando. I wonder what he'd say if we offered him a deal? He tells the truth about Davy and the fighter who died a few months ago, and Lucas will represent his daughter for free."

"We didn't kill anyone," Ethan said.

"Never said you did. But two fighters *are* dead."

A pause so long I was ready to repeat my threat when Ethan finally said, "Yes. Davy died last night."

"And you dumped the body," Savannah said.

"No, we moved him to Dr. Phillips' office where he can conduct an autopsy. As you said, this isn't the first time it's happened. In six months, we've had two deaths and one near fatality. The first time, we thought it was a fluke. It does happen, as hard as you try to avoid it. The fighter collapsed in the ring. We cleared the place out, as we did last night. Then we took him to his hotel."

"And made it look like he'd died in his sleep," I said. "Possibly from injuries sustained at the club. But with the doctor confirming he walked out, no one would blame you. You chalked it up to a freak accident."

"Until it happened again," Savannah said. "And then again."

"The second time, the fighter *did* walk out okay, and he's still walking around. But if I hadn't had an epi pen here, he'd be dead. Everyone knew he was allergic to nuts, so they figured that's what it was."

"You disagreed because he was in the ring, fighting, not sitting down to a meal that accidentally had nuts in it."

When Ethan didn't answer, I said, "You think someone's killing your fighters. The obvious reason is cheating. Poison or magic to defeat an opponent, only occasionally the results are lethal."

Tommy shook his head. "They've fought a different guy each time. In two cases, the victor would have taken the match anyway. No reason to cheat."

"So what *do* you think the problem is?" I asked.

Silence. Savannah waited five seconds this time, then stood. "Fine. You want us to figure it out for ourselves, we—"

"It's the Warners," Tommy said.

"We *suspect* it's the Warners," Ethan said. "They run—"

"A chain of fight clubs," Savannah said. "We've done our research."

The Warners owned the club in San Francisco and a half-dozen others, ranging from here to upstate Florida. They were a family of sorcerers who had once run a Cabal before being squeezed out by the big four. Now, having shed their corporate cloak, they operated everything from fight clubs to drug rings to brothels, all aimed at the supernatural market.

"When we first opened, they were fine with us," Ethan said. "We were far enough away, and our place is a dive compared to theirs. They even sent patrons and fighters our way."

"Yeah," Tommy snorted. "The ones they didn't want. We were their garbage pit. Only we wouldn't take their trash and eventually our place was cleaner than theirs. A lot cleaner."

"So you started attracting the better patrons and fighters," Savannah said. "Which is when they decided they weren't as happy having you here."

Ethan nodded. "They've offered to buy us out. Six months ago, they stopped offering…and we started having accidents."

Homeward Bound

While we were with the Gallantes, Lucas had texted to say he suspected my theory was correct. Jared had hoped to use the money he'd made at the club for a down-payment on his gambling debt. Only Tommy took the money back, so Jared's creditors beat him up. I doubt they'd meant to kill him—a corpse can't pay back anything—but add the loan shark's beating to Tommy's, and the results had been fatal.

I left that investigation to Lucas. I had a new case to work. The Gallantes had hired me to investigate the deaths at their club. I'd start by getting an unbiased view of the situation with the Warners. Eventually, that would require a trip to San Francisco. First, we needed to read through files and put out calls to contacts. The boring part, as Savannah called it. Yet she volunteered. Savannah knew that private investigation wasn't all fights and break-ins and tailing suspects, and she was determined to pull her weight.

There was, however, another reason she'd volunteer—she had contacts far more suited to researching black-market types like the Warners. Savannah cultivated a network of contacts who'd never work with me or Lucas. Former associates of her mother, they hoped to woo Savannah as an ally. Like her dark magic spells, she thinks we don't know about them. Like those spells, I hate maintaining the fiction that we don't know, but for now, it seems best.

So Savannah headed home to do her part. I stayed in Santa Cruz, but made plans for a trip of my own—to Los Angeles. Time to pay a surprise visit to my husband.

Unfortunately, I had no idea where Lucas was staying. Savannah called and hinted for details, but he didn't bite. I ran a credit card check, but there were no transactions in the last day. Ava must have been footing the bill for his hotel room, which was odd. We usually submit expenses together. But if she'd insisted, he wouldn't have argued.

Before Savannah left, she said, "Forget surprising him. Just tell him you're coming." So I called and told him Savannah was researching the Warners.

"So while she handles that, I'm free."

I paused, expecting him to ask me to join him. When he didn't respond, I said, "That means I could come there. Help you out."

"Ah."

Ah? "That's a no? Okay. I, uh, guess you're close to wrapping this up anyway."

"No, I wouldn't say that. Unfortunately."

There was a pause before the last word, as if he'd had to remind himself to say it. He hurried on, listing all the tasks he still needed to accomplish and insisting, regretfully, that he probably wouldn't be home for a few days.

Lucas was an expert liar, but I'd learned to recognize the signs when he was prevaricating.

"You're going home, then, I take it?" he said. "Today?"

"I guess so."

"Good. There should be a flight back later this afternoon. Take that, go home and rest. No need to rush off after the Warners."

I smiled as I realized where this was heading. "I don't know. If I get in early, I really should head to the office. Get caught up. Help Savannah."

"Absolutely not. You deserve a rest. Go home."

"Should I call you when I get in?"

A pause. "You can try, but I suspect I'll be out. I have several leads to follow that can only be done at night, and I may have my phone turned off."

Lying about the case being almost done. Making sure I was going home. Warning me not to expect to hear from him. Someone was planning a surprise visit of his own.

"All right then," I said. "I'll have a relaxing evening. Savannah was planning to go back to Adam's place and hang out." She'd said no such thing, but I was sure I could convince her easily enough. "She'll probably just crash there."

"Good. Excellent. You'll get a decent rest, then."

I smiled. Oh, I wasn't planning on doing much resting tonight.

I MANAGED TO get a seat on a flight heading home just over an hour later, barely squeaking through security in time. Savannah had taken my car from the airport lot, so I caught a cab and made a pit-stop at my favorite lingerie store.

I spent the next hour stocking up on supplies. I bought champagne and strawberries, plus everything I'd need for breakfast in bed. I grabbed a few more things, too—a travel book, sunscreen and a Hawaiian shirt. Then I went home and printed off pages for Maui sell-off vacations I'd bookmarked the night before. I didn't dare to actually book a vacation for us—too risky with our schedules—but this would do. I tucked the pages into a suitcase with the book, sunscreen and shirt, and hid it in our room, where I could pull it out while we were catching our breath.

Final step—change into my new bustier, panties and garters, then put on the low-cut green silk dress I usually saved for romantic dinners out. After that…well, after that, there wasn't much else to do but wait.

Savannah had e-mailed me pages on the Warners, and I was just settling in to read those when my phone blipped, telling me I had a text. I smiled and grabbed it, only to find a message from Ava, wanting me to call her ASAP.

Lucas must have left already. She was probably trying to get in touch with him before he got on the plane, tell him she urgently needed him back, only to find he'd turned off his phone early.

I considered not calling her back, but that would be petty. I should thank her. She'd highlighted hairline fractures in our marriage, which I was going to repair before the stability of the whole was in danger.

When I called, her line was busy. Had she gotten hold of Lucas? I hoped not. If she made up a plausible enough story, he'd feel obligated to go back.

I texted her and returned to reading the files. Nearly an hour later, she texted to say she was busy right now, but could I phone her in an hour? Lucas had left a message and wanted to be sure I got it.

Call in an hour? A message from Lucas? If my husband wanted to speak to me, he was quite capable of using either text or e-mail. Ava Cookson was up to something.

SAVANNAH TEXTED ME at eleven to say she had a lead on someone who owed the Warners a lot of cash. She was investigating now and we'd discuss it in the morning. I considered calling her back, but I wanted to find out what Ava was up to first. Lucas could be in a cab heading home right now, so I wanted to get this over with.

When Ava didn't answer after three rings, I almost hung up and called Savannah back. Then the line clicked and her sleepy voice said, "Hello?"

"It's Paige Winterbourne. You asked me to call."

She swore and bedsprings creaked, as if she was sitting up fast. "Oh my God, I'm so sorry. I completely forgot."

"That's fine. If it's urgent, have Lucas—"

A faint clatter cut me short. It was a sound I knew so well I could visualize it. Lucas waking, half-asleep, reaching for his glasses on the nightstand...

"Who is it?" asked a voice, one I knew just as well, and I struggled to breathe, praying I wouldn't hear—

"Your wife," came the reply, muffled, as if Ava had covered the phone.

A soft curse, then the sound of someone scrambling out of bed.

Someone? Someone? You know who's climbing out of her bed.

A murmur—Lucas's voice, words indistinguishable. Footsteps padded across the floor. A door clicked shut.

"Sorry," Ava said, coming back. "I'm not alone, which explains why I totally forgot you were calling. Totally forgot *everything*." She giggled.

I hung up.

Waking Nightmare

I sat on the sofa. Just sat there, unable to think, unable to form a thought. When I could, all I could think were two words. Not possible.

I was dreaming. I'd fallen asleep while I was waiting to call Ava, and I would wake up soon with Lucas's hand on my shoulder, his warm breath on my cheek, the faint smell of his shaving lotion…

Tears burned my eyes. I blinked them back. There had to be another explanation. He'd been in her hotel room, discussing the case. They'd fallen asleep.

On the bed? *Together?*

Maybe it wasn't a bed. They were on a couch and he'd been getting his glasses from the side-table and the creak of springs had been sofa springs.

It wasn't what it had sounded like. It couldn't be.

I called Lucas's number. As it rang, I pictured him listening to my ring tone, seeing my picture on the screen, just sitting there, waiting for voice mail—

"Hello." His voice was hesitant, as if he already regretted answering, and my insides knotted. The first tears trickled down my cheeks. I swiped them away.

"Hey." I tried to sound casual. "I thought you were out."

"I am, unfortunately." His voice had an odd echo. In a bathroom? Her bathroom, where he'd retreated after I called? "I really shouldn't talk."

Couldn't talk. That's what he meant. Wasn't ready for me. Wasn't sure if I'd heard him with her. Wasn't ready with an excuse.

"Ava called," I said. "She had a message from you, but I never did get it, so I thought I'd go straight to you."

"Message?"

A pause, and I knew there'd been no message. Of course there hadn't. She'd texted me to call in an hour because she knew by then they'd be dozing, and I'd call and she'd nudge him, accidentally of course. He'd wake and I'd hear him and I'd know.

"Perhaps she misunderstood," he went on. "There wasn't a message, so no need to worry."

Someone spoke in the background. A young woman. Lucas quickly covered the phone and murmured to her.

"Who's that?" I said.

"Just the contact I was meeting. I really should go. I'll call you in the morning."

I said goodbye, but he'd already disconnected.

No "I love you." No "Sleep well." No "I can't wait to be home." Nothing.

I sat there, phone still in hand, tears streaming down. Then I collapsed back on the sofa and sobbed until I couldn't breathe.

I gasped, wiping my face, struggling to get a grip, make a plan.

Make a *plan*? I couldn't even form a coherent thought.

Lucas had cheated on me.

Everything inside me screamed I was wrong. I had to be wrong. This was Lucas. *Lucas.*

When someone knocked, I blinked, then turned toward the front door and checked my watch. A second knock, and I realized it came from the back. A key clicked in the lock.

"Paige?" Adam called. "I need to grab a file."

When I didn't answer, he called my name again. Then his footsteps sounded in the kitchen. I held still, praying he'd think I'd gone to bed and slip past, find the file and leave. He came into the living room and saw me on the sofa.

"Paige?"

I faked a yawn. "Sorry, just dozing. What's up?"

He flicked on the light before I could stop him. I tried to turn away, but he strode over, saying, "Paige? What happened?" Then he looked at the phone still in my hand and stopped dead. "Shit. It's not— Is everything okay?"

I couldn't answer.

"It's not Lucas, right?"

Fresh tears filled my eyes. I blinked them back, but not fast enough and crouched in front of me.

"Is he hurt?"

I shook my head. "He...he slept with her. Ava."

I waited for his laugh. Not just a chuckle, but a tremendous burst of laughter that would tell me I was nuts.

Only he didn't laugh. He just sat there, looking at me, and the expression on his face wasn't shock or disbelief. It was pain.

"I'm sorry," he said.

My heart thudded against my ribs. No, this wasn't right. Adam should laugh. He should tease me about getting into the champagne early or falling asleep and having a bad dream, because clearly—*clearly*—Lucas had not cheated on me.

He hovered there, as if trying to decide something, then lowered himself beside me. He leaned forward, elbows on his knees, silent for a moment, then he twisted to meet my gaze.

"A few months ago, when you were out of town, I…" He took a deep breath. "I caught him. With someone. It wasn't anything…Well, it wasn't completely incriminating, just…"

He hesitated, then shook his head as if deciding I didn't need details.

I was misunderstanding him. I had to be. Or he'd misunderstood what he'd seen. Not Lucas. *Never* Lucas.

Adam went on. "He fell over himself insisting it wasn't what it looked like, that he was just under a lot of stress because of the Cabal stuff, and with you away, and he'd had a few drinks…"

He rubbed his chin. "I believed him. I figured he was just flirting, and me catching him was all he needed to realize how close he'd come to completely fucking up his life."

"But…Ava," I managed. "You knew she—"

"—had the hots for him. Yeah. I figured letting him go with her was a good test. If he didn't give in to temptation, then everything was okay. And if he did…?"

Adam clenched his fists and I could feel the heat radiating from them.

"Don't," I whispered.

"He doesn't deserve you, Paige. Never did. When you hooked up with him, I wondered what the hell you were thinking. But you were happy, so I didn't say anything. Then you bought this house, and he moved in and next thing you know, you're marrying the guy. He barely earned enough to cover his expenses, jetted all over the country playing crusader while you slaved at home and raised Savannah."

"It wasn't like that."

"Yeah, it was. But then he bought the office with his trust fund, so you guys had a place to work together, and I figured he was finally manning up. Then a few years later, what happens? He joins the Cabal. The *Cabal*."

"It's not like—"

"Not like that? Listen to yourself. You spent years supporting him. Then years helping build his business. And what does he do? Joins forces with the bad guys and screws around on you. Don't defend him."

I kept my mouth shut, but inside, I was still thinking, "It's not like that," because it wasn't. I'd been the one who insisted Lucas take pro bono jobs. I'd seen how much it hurt him to watch me working while he chased his dream. I'd known how hard it was to dip into his hated trust fund, but I'd known it was important, too, for him to buy the business so we could pursue our dream together. I understood why he helped with the Cabal and how much he struggled with that choice.

"We should have seen this coming," Adam went on. "As soon as he joined the Cabal. Screwing around on your wife is just part of the culture. Hell, his own mother was Benicio's mistress, and Benicio saw nothing wrong with making his bastard son the heir. A complete lack of respect for his wife."

Again, I wanted to say it wasn't like that. Benicio had made a political marriage, and ended up with a vicious woman who threatened to ruin his business in a divorce. They hadn't lived together for decades.

Adam knew all that. He'd never had a problem with it before. Never had a problem with Lucas before and certainly never said he thought I was being mistreated.

Adam was my oldest friend. Whenever he'd had issues with the guys I'd dated, he'd said so, which meant he was back-filling now, reshaping history to make me feel better. Only I didn't want him to tell me what an asshole Lucas was. I wanted sympathy and support until I'd calmed down enough to make a decision.

Adam shifted closer and put his arm around my waist. I tensed, then leaned against him, closed my eyes and let the tears fall again.

"Lucas has changed," Adam said after a few minutes. "He's not the guy you fell in love with. You know that. You've known that for a while."

His arm tightened around me. "You've grown apart. We've all seen that. He's becoming the Cabal heir, and you're becoming the heir's wife. Not his business partner. Not his confidante. Not his lover. Just his wife. You're trying to be everything he needs, but *you* haven't changed, Paige. It's all him. He's not the same guy, and you know it."

But he was. Even now, knowing what Lucas had done, I couldn't find comfort in that excuse—that he'd changed—because he hadn't. His life had changed. His work had changed. But as the Cabal sucked him in, I'd watched for any sign that it was changing him. It hadn't. He was still the guy who wanted to save the world. He'd just come to realize that it might not happen quite the way he'd thought it would. He'd learned to be flexible. He'd grown up.

I wasn't making excuses for him. None of that changed what he'd done. I'd need to deal with that, but I couldn't just say, "He's changed into a selfish jerk." Whatever had happened to us, it was more complicated than that.

Adam brushed my hair from my shoulders and held me as I cried. When he kissed the top of my head, I stiffened, but only for a second, before relaxing back against him.

"He doesn't deserve you," he said, putting his hand under my chin. He lifted my face until our eyes met. "He never did."

Adam leaned forward. His lips touched mine and I jerked back so fast I tumbled to the floor.

He gave a wry smile. "Not that scary, is it?"

He bent to help me up. I scrambled out of his way and shot to my feet, as he stared at me like a twelve-year-old who's had his heart trampled by his first crush.

I was having a nightmare. There was no doubt about it now. First Lucas sleeping with Ava. Then finding out it might not be the first time he'd cheated. And now Adam—*Adam*—making a pass at me.

Adam had never hit on me. Well, okay, once when he was thirteen, he'd tried to cop a feel, but considering our ages and my early development, I'd have been surprised if he hadn't tried that at least once. And once was all it had been.

There was no way my oldest friend just happened to be nursing a deep, unrequited love for me, and managed to hide it while working and socializing with me for years.

"Is it really that big a shock?" he said finally.

"Um, yes. Yes, it is. I'm…I'm going to go back to sleep now, and when I wake up, Lucas will be here and you'll be flirting with Savannah, and everything will be back to normal."

"Flirting with Savannah?" He looked shocked. "She's a kid, Paige. We hang out. That's it. You're the one I—"

"No, I'm not. Trust me, I'm not and we both know it."

He stepped toward me. I backed up—and smacked into the wall. He kept coming. I held up my hands.

"Stop right there, Adam. Do you remember what happened when we were kids and you tried to feel me up?"

He smiled. "How could I forget?"

"I zapped you with an energy bolt and you felt it for weeks."

The smile grew. "Some days I think I'm still feeling it."

"And do you remember what I said? That if you ever tried something like that again, I'd aim lower."

He laughed. "I remember, and I get the hint." He stepped back. "I'll give you your space, but we need to talk—"

A binding spell stopped him mid-sentence. I strode over and looked up at him, frozen in place.

"I didn't hit you with an energy bolt. I calmly moved your hand away and you got the message. We never said a word about it. No spells. No threats. I don't know who you are, but you're not Adam Vasic."

His eyes blazed copper. He lunged, and the spell snapped. I stumbled out of the way. When he kept coming, I hit him with a knockback spell. He fell back against a lamp and it crashed to the floor.

"Remember that lamp?" I said. "Remember where we bought it?"

"You honestly think I remember buying a stupid lamp?"

"No, because you aren't Adam. If you were, you couldn't have snapped that binding spell."

A humorless smile. "Face it, your spells aren't that good, babe. Especially when you're as stressed out as you are right now, which also explains why you're pulling this shit. I'm making my big confession here, laying my heart on the line and—"

"You aren't Adam."

"No? What's the explanation, then? Glamour spell? That only works if you were expecting to see him tonight, which you weren't."

"Demonic possession."

"Right, like any low-level fiend would dare possess a demon lord's son."

No matter what he said, there was no doubt that the thing talking to me wasn't Adam. He wasn't even bothering to try now, throwing off Adam's tone, his personality, his mannerisms.

I had to be sure what was going on, though, before I could do anything about it. I knew a spell that would reveal a possessing demon, but it came with a dangerous side-effect. Definitely a last resort.

"Okay, if you are Adam, tell me this. When—"

"I'm not playing that game anymore, Paige." The phone started to ring. He snatched it up and threw it across the room. "Do you know how much this hurts? We've been friends—"

"Since when?" I said. "When did we first meet? How? Who was—?"

He dove at me. I tried to swing out of the way, but he caught my arm and wrenched it, and I hit the floor, pain screaming through my shoulder.

"I don't want to hurt you," he said, coming at me again. "I just need you to sit down so I can talk—"

I caught him in another binding spell. His eyes glowed and he broke free with a snarl. I lifted my hands to launch a knockback, but he grabbed my arm, red-hot fingers searing into me. I howled in agony and he let go. I stared down at my arm, blistered and raw. Then I slammed him with an energy bolt that knocked him off his feet, and he hit the floor, convulsing.

I cast the demon reveal spell and Adam's form shimmered. His eyes blazed pure white and when they turned my way, I saw a demon. A very pissed off demon.

He struggled to his feet. I tried to smack him down with a knockback, but nothing happened. That was the side-effect— reveal the demon and your spells react as they would on a demon, which meant not at all.

Dragon's Blood & Buckthorn

I raced upstairs. Once in the bathroom, I slammed and locked the door. Then I went through the door leading into our room and locked it behind me, hoping he'd think I'd barricaded myself in the bathroom.

As the demon thumped up the stairs, the phone rang again. I thought of veering for it, but he was too close.

I snuck into our walk-in closet and eased the door shut. Then I used a spell to unlock a second door, this one leading to a cupboard barely big enough for me to squeeze into. A decent hiding place. But what I wanted was what we kept in this hidden cubby—our ritual materials.

I'd only tried demon exorcism once. Lucas was more adept at it, but even he couldn't always manage the tricky ritual.

At the thought of Lucas, I hesitated. If Adam was possessed, could Lucas be, too? No, he drank a weekly potion to guard against it. So did I. Adam was supposed to, but he swore the brew gave him a headache, reacting to his demon blood.

Besides, as Adam argued, demons rarely possessed the children of lords. Too many political implications.

But even if Lucas *wasn't* possessed, maybe this was still connected and he hadn't really—

A thud as the demon pounded on the bathroom door. "Come out, you little bitch! I made a bargain and I'm damned well going to keep my end of it."

I started gathering everything I'd need. Dragon's blood, buckthorn— I pulled the box for buckthorn off the shelf. It was empty.

Empty? Who the hell would leave—

Savannah.

Goddamn it! Taking the last piece of bread and not putting it on the grocery list was bad enough. We were going to have a talk about this. Right after I had a talk about Adam not drinking his anti-possession brew.

"Do you think I can't break this door down? You have three seconds to come out, or that's not all I'm breaking!"

Okay, forget Savannah and Adam. First, I had to survive long enough to chew them out.

I grabbed more boxes from the shelves, ripping off lids, praying Savannah had just misplaced the buckthorn.

"Three, two, one..." A crash as he kicked in the bathroom door.

Face it, I wasn't finding the buckthorn. Not in time anyway. What other ritual could I use? Would rituals work against him if my spells didn't? What if—?

"Where the hell are you hiding, witch?"

His footsteps thundered down the hall.

I grabbed vervain from the shelf. It was for banishing ghosts, but it might weaken the demon enough for my spells to work.

My hands trembled as I poured the dried herbs into a censer. As the demon thumped into the bedroom, I lit the censer. He went straight for the closet, and ripped open the door.

A grunt, as if he could sense me inside, but couldn't figure out where I was hiding. Hangers clicked as he searched. Then, with another grunt, he found the inner door. He kicked it in. Splinters rained down on me as I blew hard on the vervain, sending a cloud of smoke into his face.

The demon coughed and swatted at it. The yellow glow in his eyes dimmed.

"Vervain?" he said. "Do you think I'm some lowly shade to be banished with—"

I hit him with a knockback. He barely teetered, but his eyes widened as he realized I'd weakened his immunity.

I launched an energy bolt, then a knockback, then another bolt and he stumbled back, dazed. I hit him again—this time with my hands—and dodged past him into the bedroom.

"You're only going to piss me off, witch," he yelled as he came after me. "And that's not something you want—"

He stopped. Still running, I glanced back to see him frozen in place. Then I smacked into Savannah as she rounded the top of the stairs.

"That's not—" I began.

"Adam. Yeah, I know. He was acting weird at the office. Avoiding me, which is weird for Adam. I knew something was up, but when I went to confront him, I found myself trapped. Bastard jammed a chair under the doorknob. Unlock spells don't really work well on that. I tried calling you, in case he was coming here, but I guess he'd already arrived." She glanced over at me. "He hasn't been taking his anti-possession brew, has he?"

"Apparently not. I cast a demon reveal, thinking I could get into the storeroom and whip up the exorcism potion. Seems we're out of buckthorn."

She winced. "Sorry. It's downstairs in the kitchen cupboard."

"Why would you—?" I shook my head. "Fine. Let's tie this guy up, and I'll get the buckthorn."

SAVANNAH HAD PUT the herbs in the tea cupboard, reasoning that it looked enough like tea leaves not to concern any human guests. As for why she'd needed it in the kitchen at all, I wasn't going to ask.

I headed upstairs. All was silent up there, meaning the demon was still locked in Savannah's binding spell.

I was starting down the hall when the stairs creaked behind me. Before I could turn, something cold went around my neck. I grabbed it and spun, lashing out with a knockback spell that sent my attacker slamming into the wall.

"Lucas?"

"Your defensive reaction has improved. Apparently, sneaking up to deliver a gift is no longer such a wise idea."

"Gift?" I looked down at my hand. What I'd grabbed was a necklace with an engraved red stone for a pendant.

"A carnelian amulet of Hamiah," he said. "I know you've been looking for one."

I stared at it and my first thought was: *It's an apology. He thinks he can buy me off with baubles.* But then I looked up at him, and he smiled, and I knew whatever I'd heard on the phone had been an illusion. Counterfeit magic to convince me my husband had been unfaithful.

I lifted onto my tiptoes and kissed him. He kissed me back with no hesitation, no surprise, no sign that I'd have any reason *not* to welcome him home.

"Oh my God!"

Savannah's voice made us jump apart. She strode down the hall, gaze fixed on Lucas's shirt. I followed it to see a crimson stain spreading across it. He looked down and touched it.

"You're hurt," I said. "How—?"

He cut me off by pressing his stained fingers to my lips. Sweet and fruity.

"Strawberry jam?" I said.

"Spread, actually. Another gift. Your knockback must have broken the jar in my pocket."

"Strawberry spread?" Savannah said. "Why would you—?" She stopped and lifted her hands. "Dumb question and I don't want to hear the answer."

"Nor was I going to provide it. So—"

A muffled sound from the bedroom cut him off.

"Shit," Savannah said. "Binding spell broke."

She hurried in to recast it. Before I could explain, Lucas strode to the bedroom door. He looked at what appeared to be Adam, bound, gagged and sitting on our bed.

"Ah," Lucas said. "Seems I interrupted something. My apologies."

Savannah laughed. "Only you would walk in on this and apologize. It's not what it looks like."

"It's not demonic possession?"

She laughed again. "And only you would jump to that conclusion."

"Yes, it's possession," I said. "Someone sent him here to seduce me—"

Savannah made choking noises.

"It didn't work," I said.

"Well, duh. I just mean…eww. Adam is not going to live this one down."

"I'm sure he won't. But before we bring him back, we need to find out who sent the demon."

"Someone who's not very bright," Savannah said. "Sending anyone to seduce you would be a waste of time. But Adam?" She shook her head. "Time to get some answers."

Contract Negotiations

*S*avannah walked over and yanked the gag off the demon. "Okay, who's the dumb-ass who sent you to possess Adam and seduce Paige?"

The demon pressed his lips together and glowered at us.

"I asked you a question," Savannah said.

"Let's forget *who* for now," I said. "*Why* did someone want you to seduce me?"

Again, he didn't answer. Savannah lifted her hands to hit him with a spell, then quickly lowered them, as if she'd remembered it was Adam's body she was about to blast. He'd suffer the consequences when he returned.

"We should begin the exorcism," Lucas said. "Clearly, he isn't going to reveal his employer's identity."

"Employer?" the demon said.

"My apologies. A poor choice of words, as you are not receiving financial compensation. Whoever holds the chit against you, I mean. Whomever you fear if you break this obligation."

"I fear no one. And I answer to no one."

As Lucas kept baiting him, I looked at the stain on his shirt. He'd come home early to surprise me. There was no way he'd even been in Los Angeles when I'd called Ava.

I cast a privacy spell so I could speak to him without being overheard. "How did you get back so fast? I talked to you less than an hour ago."

I'm sure he wondered why I was interrupting to ask this, but I had a feeling the answers might help us get some from the demon.

He cast his own privacy spell. "My father was in L.A. for meetings with the Nasts so," he gave a faint smile, "I borrowed the keys to his jet. I was almost here when you called."

That explained the hollow sound—he'd been on a plane. It also explained the young woman talking in the background—the flight attendant.

Ava hadn't sent those messages hoping I'd catch her in bed with Lucas. She'd known that wasn't happening. She'd sent them so I'd catch her in bed with someone who could impersonate Lucas.

I turned to the demon. "It was Ava Cookson, wasn't it? She wanted me to think Lucas had cheated, then you'd come over to console me."

"She thought she could convince you that Lucas had screwed around?" Savannah snorted. "She's even dumber than she looked."

I felt Lucas's gaze on me. He knew I'd fallen for it. Shame washed over me and I looked away.

"I don't doubt Ava's involved," Lucas said. "But not as the mastermind. She's simply a pawn. Like him." A dismissive wave at the demon.

The demon's eyes blazed yellow. "I'm nobody's pawn."

"No? Then if you don't fear repercussions, tell me who summoned you."

"You're supposed to be a genius," the demon said. "You figure it out."

That's what he wanted. Us to figure it out. Otherwise, he could have left Adam's body the minute Savannah bound it. He wanted to negotiate, but the contract that bound him forbade him from revealing who'd made it.

"We know that Ava's brother did die," I said. "That was a matter of public record. And we know he was at the Gallantes' fight club, although I doubt they killed him."

"They didn't," Lucas said. "As you suspected, he was killed by his human debtors. I verified that today and believe Ava knew it all along. However, her case did have potential supernatural overtones. It was an excuse to hire me, and put the plan in action."

"So the plan was just to make Paige think Lucas had been unfaithful," Savannah said. "Drive her into the arms of her sexy guy friend. But why?"

"Ava was chosen for a reason, wasn't she?" I said to the demon. "Presumably, it would have been easier to convince me Lucas cheated if it was with someone older and smarter. But whoever hired the demon chose Ava because he wanted us investigating the Gallantes' fight club. He wanted us there the night a fighter died."

"Seems the little woman is a better detective than you," the demon said to Lucas.

"No," I said. "I'm just better at thinking out loud."

"Clearly, your assumption is correct, then," Lucas said. "Someone wanted Adam to seduce you *and* wanted us investigating the Gallantes. I fail to see how the first part ties into the second, but if the Warners are orchestrating the deaths to put the Gallantes out of business, then they would be the obvious suspects."

"Or someone who owes the Warners a whole lot of money," Savannah said. "Who might do this for them in return for his debt."

"Possibly," Lucas said. "However—"

"Remember that message I sent you?" Savannah said to me. "I know who owes the Warners. Someone with the clout to call a demon. Someone who'd love to see Lucas suffer as a bonus. Someone who's nasty as hell, but not quite bright enough to pull this off."

"Carlos," Lucas said.

Savannah nodded. She turned to the demon. "Blink twice for no. Once for yes."

He blinked once.

WE HAD TO strike a deal with the demon to get him to fill in the blanks. Ten years ago, I'd have been horrified at the suggestion. But Lucas wasn't the only one who'd learned to be flexible. Demons could be bargained with, if you knew what you were doing. Lucas did.

The agreement was simple. He'd tell us the details and in return, we agreed to stand as his defense and character witnesses, should Carlos accuse him of breaking his bargain. We'd support his claim that Carlos had sent him on an impossible mission. Sounded silly, but demons are like any other contract worker. If they break a deal, no one's going to call them back.

Once we agreed, the demon told his story. Carlos owed the Warners for debts rung up at their fight clubs. They came to him with an offer—put the Gallantes out of business and they'd forget the debt. I'm sure they figured he'd use his Cabal clout to do that, but he couldn't when the Gallantes' club was in Nast territory. So he hired someone to inject fighters with poison during a pre-game backslap from a supporter.

It would have worked eventually, but Carlos was impatient. Besides, he had another, more irritating thorn in his side to worry about: Lucas. Then, while he was in L.A. on business, he had a one-night stand with a half-demon who told him about her own experience with the Gallantes. With that, Carlos saw the solution to both problems. Hire Ava to get us on the case and pretend to seduce Lucas.

Yes, *pretend* to seduce him. Carlos knew his half-brother wouldn't actually cheat on me. The point was simply to send me into Adam's arms. Lucas would be crushed and would blame himself, thinking his involvement in the Cabal had driven me away. To keep me, he'd leave the Cabal. Carlos was sure of it.

After the demon finished his story, we returned Adam to his body. I decided to let Savannah explain what had happened. It was a little too embarrassing, coming from me. Lucas and I went downstairs and he insisted on tending to my burned arm. As he bandaged it, I fingered the amulet now around my neck.

"Thank you," I said after a few minutes. "For this."

He nodded and finished binding my arm before he said, "Did you really think I'd been unfaithful?"

"No, but the proof seemed to be there and I…I guess I didn't want to be one of those women who sees the signs and pretends she doesn't. Anyway, Carlos's plan didn't work. That demon didn't get anywhere with me."

"Of course not."

I know he didn't mean those words—spoken with such certainty—to sting. But they did. Even Carlos—never known for his brains—was astute enough to realize Lucas wouldn't cheat. Yet he believed he could convince me he had, and he'd been right.

I thought about Ethan Gallante and remembered what he'd told his blackmailer, "You can bring me all the evidence you want; my answer will remain the same. I trust my brother." I thought I'd have said the same thing about my husband. But I'd let my problems with the Cabal wear down my confidence and my trust, and the shame of that burned.

"I'm sorry," I said as Lucas sat beside me on the couch.

"Don't be. If you thought there was a possibility, then we have a problem. I've known that for a while."

"There's no problem," I said. "Sure, things are tough, but you and I are—"

He twisted to face me. "Paige, please. Don't keep saying everything's all right. Don't keep acting like it is. We both know it's not, but I can't address the problem when you won't admit there is one."

"I—"

"You're struggling. You're feeling left behind and left out. But you don't want to upset me, and you want to handle it on your own. You think if you keep working at it, the Cabal will realize you're a valuable asset."

Nailed it on the first try.

His voice softened. "That's not going to happen, Paige. I thought it would. I hoped it would. But it's not."

"And it won't. I'm a woman, I'm a witch and I'm married to the guy they don't want leading their company."

The demon had tried to seduce me by insisting Lucas was no longer the man I'd married. Part of me did grieve for the life we'd lost when his brothers died. I understood why Lucas needed to be part of the Cabal, but I still grieved.

Yet even when I'd wanted to hate Lucas, I'd recognized the demon's lies for what they were. My life had changed; my husband hadn't.

Our marriage *was* in trouble. Pretending it wasn't would only make things worse.

"I'm leaving the Cabal," Lucas said.

I shook my head. "We can handle Carlos. I have some ideas. He won't try anything like this—"

"Carlos has nothing to do with it. It's not working out. I need to make a choice. Maybe I'm being selfish, but I choose you." He leaned over, lips brushing mine as he whispered, "I always choose you."

Only, he couldn't. As strong as Benicio was for his age, the stress of preparing a new heir to fight Carlos would be too much. In the meantime, his search would leave the Cabal vulnerable. The Nasts, sensing weakness, would strike.

The supernatural world needed the Cortez Cabal to balance the evil of the Nasts and St. Clouds. The Cortez Cabal needed Benicio. Benicio needed Lucas. Wishing it wasn't so wouldn't change that.

"You can't," I said.

He squared his shoulders. "Yes, I can, and I—"

"No, you can't. The ball is in my court on this one. You're right, I need to stop pretending nothing's wrong. And stop pretending it's going to change."

"You shouldn't—"

"But I will. Suck it up and deal. That's what I have to do." I looked over at him. "When I was in Miami this week, after the meeting, one of the employees talked to me. She'd just been promoted to management, and was having a problem. The other managers hold weekly meetings at a strip club, which means she's missing out. She wanted my advice. I told her she had two choices. One, take it over their heads and insist they move the meetings. Two, go to the meetings anyway. I suggested the latter."

Lucas chuckled. "They'd probably be so embarrassed that they'd change the venue."

"Maybe. But whether they did or not, the point is she wouldn't miss the meetings. She agreed and thanked me. She said there wasn't anyone else for her to talk to. I've been butting my head against their damned glass ceiling, determined to make a difference. But I *did* make a difference on that trip. I was just too focused on the big win to celebrate the small one. That's where I can do some good. Helping anyone who feels like an outsider, wants to talk to someone who isn't a Cortez, isn't a sorcerer."

"You're right that the Cabal could use you as an ombudsman for employees who feel disenfranchised, but I don't want you to feel you're settling—"

"I never settle. I just lower my oversized expectations. I've always aimed too high, first with the Coven, then the council, now with this. I've only ever set my sights on the best once and gotten it." I kissed him. "Can't expect to get that lucky ever again."

He pulled me to him and we sank into the cushions. Then Adam and Savannah's voices sounded in the hall.

"Better take a rain check," I said. "They're going to want to know what we plan to do about Carlos. Like I said, I have an idea…"

Maintaining the Charade

$\mathcal{L}$ucas and I went to Miami. It had been months since we'd gone anywhere together. I'd told myself with recent cases that it made more sense for us to split our resources. A lie. Smarting from the Cabal's rejection, my confidence had needed the boost of succeeding on my own.

I realized my mistake now. Working alone hadn't bolstered my confidence; it only hammered a wedge between us. So we flew to Miami together, even if I didn't need to be there.

While I stayed at the hotel, Lucas went in to the office early, taking our new spy camera so I could watch my plan unfold. He spoke to his father first. He didn't tell him what happened. Lucas had never tattled on his half-brothers, even when they'd tormented him as a boy. He just said he'd come to do some work. And was Benicio free for lunch? He'd like to discuss that offer to buy him a condo in Miami.

Flying halfway across the country to "do some work?" Wanting to discuss the condo, after refusing to consider it for years? It was odd. Very odd, and I'm sure Benicio wondered what was up…which was exactly the point.

One of Carlos's sycophants would be quick to tell him that Lucas was in the office, and had met with their father. Carlos would go straight to Benicio, find out what Lucas had said and then…

Lucas's office door banged open, his secretary fluttering in behind Carlos, motioning that he'd barged past her. I watched the scene through the camera.

Carlos parked himself in front of Lucas's desk. The first time I met Carlos, I had to admit he was the most attractive of the Cortez brothers. Over the years, his looks had faded—too many drugs, too much alcohol, too many other habits I preferred not to think about. Since his brothers' deaths, he'd cleaned up the dope and booze, but those were really the least of his sins, and that dissolute look had hardened into something a lot more dangerous.

"What the hell are you doing here?" Carlos said.

"Working."

Carlos peered at him. While Lucas looked perfectly presentable, he wasn't his usual pressed and polished self. His chin bore shaving nicks. His hair looked unwashed. His clothing was rumpled.

Carlos smiled. "You're not having lunch with Dad to talk about the condo. You only said that so he wouldn't worry. You're going to tell him you're leaving."

"Leaving?"

"The Cabal. You're here to clean out your desk." He tried to look thoughtful. "It's Paige, isn't it? Something happened with Paige."

Lucas blinked in feigned surprise, then shuffled papers. "I prefer not to discuss it."

"Ah, so I'm right. Problems at home, huh? Not like we didn't all see this coming. So you're telling Dad that you're leaving—"

"Staying."

Now it was Carlos's turn to blink.

Lucas straightened the papers. "I'm here to tell him that I'm staying. My marriage is over, so I see no reason to maintain this charade."

After a moment, Carlos managed a strangled, "What?"

"The Cabal needs me. You can't be expected to cover both Hector's and William's jobs. I'm fooling myself taking on minor assignments and thinking that helps. It doesn't. I need to be here, and the only thing holding me back was Paige. She hated me working for the Cabal. Now that my marriage has ended..." His jaw tightened, eyes cooling. "It appears to be time for a fresh start. I'll be accepting my role as heir."

"Wh-what happened?" A split-second pause. "Did she find someone else? Because if she did, I'm sure it's not what you think. Just a one-time thing. It happens. No need to—"

"Paige has not been unfaithful. Apparently, she thinks I have been. She kicked me out."

I swore I could hear Carlos's sigh of relief. His plan had gone awry, but this could be fixed.

"I'm sure it's a misunderstand—"

"It's an excuse," Lucas cut in. "She's been unhappy for months. I've tried to fix the problem, but obviously, she doesn't want it fixed, so she's concocted this wild story—"

"Are you sure it's a story? What does she think happened?"

"I have no idea. The conversation never went that far."

Carlos strode over to the coat rack and picked up Lucas's jacket and bag. "Paige isn't making up stories. Some gold-digger slut has set you up. Happens to me all the time."

"I don't think—"

"Just go home. Talk to her. You'll work this out. You don't really want to be here."

Lucas looked around, undecided, and in the silence that followed, I knew what Carlos was thinking. He'd made a fatal miscalculation. If Lucas lost me, he wouldn't fall apart. He'd grieve in his own way, by throwing himself into work. Without me to remind him of his goals, he'd fulfill Benicio's greatest dream and Carlos's greatest nightmare. He'd become a true heir.

Bullshit, of course. Lucas didn't need me to keep him straight. But as Lucas hesitated, it only confirmed Carlos's fears.

"Go on," Carlos said. "At least try. You owe your marriage that much. Hear her out. See if it can be saved. You still love her, right?"

Lucas hesitated so long I swore I could hear Carlos's heart pound. Then he said, "All right," and took his coat.

AFTER CARLOS LEFT, Lucas called me.

"Well played," I said.

"It was your script," he said. "Somehow, I don't think we'll need to worry about Carlos trying to break us up again."

"I hope not. So the next step is to foil his plan with the Gallantes."

"That will be a simple matter of exposing it. We'll head to Santa Cruz later. In the meantime, I suspect I can't wriggle out of lunch with my father."

"You shouldn't. And you might want to take his condo offer. I know we've discussed it. Go ahead and accept. That'll keep Carlos on his toes, thinking you're planning for a possible marriage failure."

"Agreed. Lunch, however, isn't for a few hours. Any thoughts on how we might fill them?"

"Oh, I have a few ideas."

"I'll be right there."

I smiled and hung up the phone. Things weren't back to normal yet. That would take work. But we'd get through it. I'd make sure of that, starting with a little Hawaiian getaway for two.